Potluck: Stories That Taste Like Hawai'i

Potluck:
Stories That Taste Like Hawai'i

Catherine Bridges Tarleton

Honolulu, Hawai'i

Printed in the United States of America

Library of Congress Control Number: 2001135349

Catherine Bridges Tarleton
Potluck: Stories That Taste Like Hawai'i

ISBN: 0-9662945-4-8

Book design and illustration by Leigh Morrison

Contents

ACKNOWLEDGMENTS

Barbara Hastings made it happen. Thank you very much.

And thanks to all the "goddesses" at Hastings & Pleadwell and to Goodale Publishing.

This book was written with friends in mind, start to finish, which is the best route anywhere. Particular appreciation goes to those who contributed their expertise to my Hawai'i potluck experience: "Chef Scampi" Larry Doran, Sr., Karen Johnson Kishimoto, Elizabeth Myklebust Moiha, Shelly Kealohalani Wakamatsu Pelfrey, Sister M. Rose Bernard (Catharine Tarleton).

And of course Mom, who did the best she could with me. Don't blame her.

Thanks to *Bamboo Ridge* which originally published "The Fishing Club" in The Best of Honolulu Fiction (1999). And, to an urban O'ahu magazine for incentive to keep writing—even if Goodale wouldn't let me subtitle my book: All the Losers of the Honolulu Fiction Contest.

To all my coaches, readers and tasters, positive and negative—and Dwight who's always been all of the above—Mahalo nui.

"Tell me what you eat, and I shall tell you what you are."
—*Anthelme Brillat-Savarin, La Physiologie du Gout, Aphorisms*

PULAKAUMAKA
(Obsession)

I try to call Hawai'i but Hawai'i never calls back.

I try to call Hawai'i from the Pentagon bus station, with my ass on the freezing granite bench and my feet in a puddle. It is sleeting. Everyone has a cold. Everyone has a shred of a tissue in front of their nose. And there is no such thing as sunshine.

I try to call Hawai'i from the Metro at National Airport, where there are no colors and no smiles and everything stinks like exhaust or exhaustion. I am on my way to work at the Banquet Department of the Vista International Hotel, but some people at the Metro stop at National Airport are going to Hawai'i today, and I could stow away. They have aloha shirts and sunscreen in their suitcases; they will be drinking *mai tai* by the time I'm home from work. In hurricane glasses. With pineapple spears and paper umbrellas and plastic palm-tree swizzle sticks.

Maybe they will bring one back for me.

Sometimes I get a busy signal.

I try to call Hawai'i from the car phone when I am stuck in traffic. Screaming at the lights and idiots. Screaming at the cold defrost that makes the window fog worse and the stupid sticking lighter and the smartass D.J. with too many opinions and the rattlesnake voice.

I try to call Hawai'i from the Giant Food store to hear a human sound that isn't ambushed by beeping scanners and screeching children wanting things they shouldn't have as their glazed-over mothers drift up and back and into lines.

Sometimes I get recordings, which is not too bad, and I listen to the steel guitars six thousand miles away. I listen to the Brothers Caz who never get old and are always headed back home, in the islands, back home, in the islands. It eases the need a little. It makes my left ear warm.

Sometimes an operator says *aloha* and *mahalo* for calling the 800 number for some hotel chain to ask about room rates and job openings and just to hear the sound of Hawai'i's voice. As soon as I hang up I replay the tape in my brain over and over until every word is burned in solid state, then I dial again to hear *aloha* and *mahalo* and *aloha* and *mahalo* for calling. Until I believe it.

I try to call Hawai'i to have something sent. I try to tell the salesman on the telephone I have to have it overnight, need it sent by UPS or FedEx, by tomorrow. But he doesn't understand.

I try to order mac nuts or papaya or a *lei* or one of those beautiful coconut bowls. Bowls polished as smooth as a waterfall-worn stone at the end of the river before it goes into the ocean in Hilo. In winter. Where surfers look out for those waves you will never forget.

And the guy on the telephone tells me you cannot put that into a bowl, but I try to explain that whatever it is will be just fine with me as long as I get it. Tomorrow. Anything from Hawai'i. To save my life.

I try calling back when he hangs up on me. I try to call back but Hawai'i is busy.

I try to call Hawai'i from my desk at the Banquet Department. I'm surrounded by computers and commuters and all I can think is if I don't get Hawai'i on the telephone in the next five minutes

I am going to drop dead. And before I die I am going to throw this Alzheimer's-ridden printer through the wall of this windowless office and take off all my clothes and go tearing like a shark bite through the continental breakfast of the Association of Federal State and County Municipal Employees.

My boss looks at me and asks for the menu for the Moslem wedding or the Gold Bat Mitzvah or the Jackson Cotillion and I look at him and start to chant. Possessed by the consciousness of Madame Pele, I succumb to spontaneous combustion. I turn him into a wild boar and curl the ends of his moustache into tusks and watch him squeal and snort and paw at patterns in the carpet.

If I can get through the busy busy busy busy signal, I will beg Hawai'i to take me away. From everything gray and everything boring and everything freezing and sodden and awful. Then I will tell Hawai'i that I want, I deserve, and I need to be there, need to be. And that I will quit smoking if, lose twenty pounds if, stop all the crying if if if if the place will take me in. I will do whatever Hawai'i wants, and I will be whatever Hawai'i wants me to be. In Hawai'i, I can.

In Hawai'i, I can paint and play music. I can make movies. I can have babies, and cook fish and rice, and take photographs with a tripod or a cable release or something like that. I can dance *hula kahiko* in moonlight. I can make everything as it should be. I can be in the right place at the right time. I can make it the right place at the right time.

In Hawai'i, I can lie in the sand and vibrate with the rhythm of surf and earthquakes. I can practice that. I can get so good at it I feel *tsunami* coming and I run to warn the children. And we all survive.

In Hawai'i, I can learn photosynthesis. I can live like a plant. I can water myself in the rain. I can survive un-uprooted, like the sugar cane, the hurricane. I can take it. Hawai'i can dish it out. Plate lunch.

In Hawai'i, I can walk on rocks, walk on water, walk on clouds to the top of Mauna Kea. Bend down and look backwards through the telescopes into the heart of the mountain and watch it beat. It is a drum. Hawai'i's heart is a drum.

(And I will also make drums from office equipment and beat them as a daily ritual.)

In Hawai'i, I will eat mangos three meals a day. I will build a house in a mango tree and bathe in mango puree. I will live with the mango tribe and run with the mango herd and howl at the mango moon with a mouthful of mango dripping down my chin like blood from the mango vampire's desperate hunger.

Please please please, oh, call me back, oh please Hawai'i, call. I send a psychic smoke signal. I clear my—breathing deeply—mind. I pray. To all the four gods and the forty, the four hundred and four thousand and the forty thousand, the four hundred thousand million billion gods. Please. The gods of all Hawai'i and of Washington, DC. The gods of mango. The gods of the Jackson Cotillion and the Pentagon and the frozen granite and the Giant Food and the blessed blessed telephone and AT&T. And all the gods of all of me. Please.

Please.

I put a *ti* leaf on my forehead and I drink a cup of Kona coffee, black. Thinking oh Hawai'i, oh Hawai'i, oh Hawai'i, please call me back.

Where did a *ti* leaf come from? Am I finally insane?

Unless it's sent by *menehune*. FedEx. Unless it grew from the red and green chunks of whatever it was that came in the mail in the stupid plastic pouch from the Hawai'i Visitors Bureau with smiling *hula* dancers on the package and the Department of Agriculture stamp of approval. Which I stuck in my house plants, and they never grew but I was afraid to throw them away, anyway.

Unless it is not here at all and I am now hallucinating from Hawai'i deprivation.

Unless it is here and I am not.

Unless I am finally there.

Here. In Hawai'i.

EVERYTHING I NEED TO KNOW ABOUT LIFE I LEARNED FROM POTLUCK

"We're having potluck on Tuesday," said my boss. "For the January birthdays." She nodded at the paper on her desk. "What do I sign you up for?"

Oh no.

Potluck. The Initiation. What do I bring to the table here? What am I willing to expose to the taste buds and scrutiny of an office full of veterans of the ancient competition of the kitchen? Do I shoot for something expensive and impressive? Should I make the commitment of lasagne, or express humility with oatmeal cookies? Do I have the right container? Am I ready for this?

"Side dish," I said.

Monday night, I made a nice light pasta salad with rotini and fresh broccoli, black olives, a little basil and onion, olive oil. I spooned it into a plastic bowl. I took it to work, forgot the serving spoon, and put it on the table with the Tupperwares and foil-covered dishes.

All morning, wonderful smells wandered into my office like people with nothing to do. Ginger, *teriyaki*, something salty and mysterious. More dishes came in; more desks were cleared to make room and everyone was checking out the food. I heard fragments of conversation that made very little sense to me.

"Is this your Auntie's butter *mochi*?" asked Pua, the front desk clerk who knew everyone and everything cooking.

"No, it's the microwave kind," said Herman. He was a small-ish Asian-looking man who did his best to make me feel at home. "What did you bring?"

"Oh, I didn't have time to cook," said Pua. "I just went to the Dai-Zen. Oh look, somebody brought *kamaboko*. I don't feel so bad."

"Where's the rice?" asked Sarah, a tiny Filipina, ninety pounds soaking wet. "I brought pork and peas. Make some room."

"They'll bring rice up from the kitchen," said Pua. "Don't worry. Look at the Jell-O. Who has time to do all that? Must be Angela. Her children are grown."

It went on and on.

About ten o'clock, nobody could wait any longer. They start-ed taking the covers off and passing out plates. I went in to the lunchroom, picked up a segmented cardboard plate and a plas-tic fork instead of the wooden chopsticks wrapped in paper. There was an amazing display of food and I was starving.

But I didn't know what anything was.

There was a plate of big green checkers that seemed to be rice rolled up in Christmas paper with tuna fish inside. There was a white box with something squishy and damp, like corners of manila envelopes stuffed with rice and sawdust. A plastic bowl of *tofu*, some kind of fish and what looked like weeds sat by a plate of taupe-colored vegetables that wiggled like rubber bands. An oblong dish in a quilted cozy steamed with brown shreds and green peas next to a square casserole of basically bones in sauce. There was an aluminum foil chafer of plain white rice, with another one waiting on the side. Colorful Tupperwares and Rubbermaids displayed slices of potatoes that were actually pur-ple, incredible rainbow-layered Jell-O cut into little squares and something that looked like mashed potatoes but smelled like custard. Other mysterious foodstuffs lined every horizontal surface, inviting us to dig in.

There was my pasta salad. Untouched.

I was two months new from Virginia where potlucks, which we called covered-dish suppers, were largely church affairs and were for the most part parades of casseroles and desserts. Macaroni and cheese, meatball stroganoff, cupcakes. This was Klingon food.

"What's that?" Herman asked me.

"Pasta salad," I said.

"Oh," he said. "I had that before in Las Vegas." He made a big pile on his plate with the little plastic fork. "Sarah," he said. "Try some of her pasta salad." He put some on her plate, and Pua's too.

"Mmm," they all said. "How you make this?"

I told them what was in it.

Sarah said, "Like macaroni salad but no mayonnaise?"

"Yeah, I guess," I said.

"Mmm," they all said again, politely.

Herman asked, "You like Filipino food?"

"I don't know," I said.

"Here." He put some of the brown stuff on my plate. "Sarah made this. Pork and peas. Try."

They loaded up my plate. They told me what everything was. I learned about cone *sushi* and oxtail and *gobo*. They had to call Auntie May into the room to tell me about the *sushi* roll because she had some way of frying the tuna in sugar and *shoyu* that made all the difference.

I took home three-fourths of the pasta salad. We had it for dinner.

From the mainland, you think of Hawai'i as a place where

everyone eats fresh fish all the time. Where tanned bodies stroll down salad bars positioned under the trees to catch the mangos as they drop onto your plate. Simple, fresh Edenic nourishment. Nothing prepares you for the complex cultural experience of potluck.

I resolved to meet the challenge.

In February, I made banana muffins. I mashed fresh bananas with a potato ricer and beat in plenty of butter and nuts. I baked them in those little paper cups, and when the first batch came out, I arranged them in rows in a foil-lined soda case. While the rest baked, 'til one in the morning, I cleaned up. The last thing to wash was the potato ricer. It was missing a screw.

Oh my God.

I looked at the muffins, beautiful, brown and buttery on the counter. I searched the kitchen sink and felt all around the disposal. Nothing.

I looked at the muffins again.

They were so nice.

They were probably fine. The screw had probably been gone for months and I just didn't notice.

Then I had this awful vision of my boss spitting fragments of tooth into her plate, of Herman giving Pua the Heimlich maneuver and my screw ejecting onto the floor.

I threw them out. In the morning I bought paper plates.

In March, I tried to make spinach rolls but the filling was too soft and the knife was too dull, so the stuff squished out of either end like a two-headed caulking gun. I gave up, scraped off the tortillas, and called it dip. The next morning I bought chips.

In April we had a picnic, and I packed the Playmate cooler with ice and assorted bagels with flavored cream cheeses cut in little neat wedges. But at lunchtime, while everybody else was eating Korean chicken and rice balls, I was draining water out of Ziploc bags of goo and trying to avoid explanation.

In May, I brought Hawaiian Sun juice.

In June, I brought paper plates, again.

The rest of the summer was hopeless. The fern shoots stayed hairy no matter how long I cooked them. The spring rolls refused to hold together. The Jell-O layers slid over each other like a fruity orgy. You could never tell when the *char siu* chicken was cooked.

I studied. I went to the library. I learned there are no recipes for *sushi* roll, that it must be part of the oral history in secret Hawai'i potluck societies. I bought one of those spiral-bound church lady cookbooks in a coffee shop in Na'alehu, with recipes for *kālua* pig (Dig a pit for a 300 lb. hog) and lye-peeled guava shells (Wear long heavy rubber gloves). Way too scary.

I went into the field. I never said no to a Filipino wedding, Hawaiian baby *lū'au*, *paniolo* branding, Chinese New Year or any kind of birthday party. I helped my girlfriend and her Japanese mother-in-law slice Spam and mash it in the lucite press to make *musubi* for soccer day. I practiced with chopsticks. I went to countless barbecues where barbecue was never served and had Japanese oysters and mountain oysters. I learned you can cook almost any food on a *hibachi*, but baked beans are not on the menu. Neither is corn on the cob.

And I ate. I ate everything. I learned that mayonnaise makes everything palatable, that any marinade is OK for any meat as long as it contains ginger and *shoyu*. I learned that not all *saimin* is the same and one package is never enough. I learned the difference between microwave *mochi* and the real thing, that *mana-*

pua is one of the greatest inventions in the world, and crack seed doesn't necessarily have seeds or cracks.

I ate *kim chee* with hamburgers and chili on spaghetti with mayonnaise. I ate shave ice with ice cream in the middle and beans in the middle of that. I ate *loco moco* and *miso* soup and *wasabi* peas and cuttlefish. I ate *sashimi* and real *sushi* and Saloon Pilot crackers with butter and guava jam. I learned that everything tastes better with beer.

I gained thirty pounds. I waddled to work in ever larger *mu'u-mu'u* on potluck days. And whatever I cooked I took home.

Oh, people were nice. They suggested fishcake and said we really could use some more napkins.

But I knew. My months of research were useless. I was no closer to being local than pasta salad. Sure, I knew to buy *lū'au* plates instead of round ones, chopsticks along with the forks, and that *shoyu* and soy sauce were the same thing. But I still harbored a deep resentment against this mystery system that left me battered with inadequacy and fried by failure.

It was a dark time.

I tried everything. I cheated. I bought *dim sum* from the deli and put them in my container. I tried to bribe my friend Christine to cook her chicken *hekka* for me. She refused.

"It's not about the food," she said.

"Is that supposed to be Zen or something?" I asked. "Of course it's about the food," I said. "Everything over here is about food. And I just don't understand." I sniffed. "I follow the instructions on the recipes. I do it just like everybody else. I've eaten everything and practiced everything and still nobody eats what I cook and I always bring my dishes home."

She patted me on the shoulder. "Let's start with the rice," she said. "First you have to have the right pot." She dug into her cabinets and pulled out a glass saucepan with a lid. "Like this. So you can see when the water disappears. Don't take the lid off until it does." She scooped out rice from a twenty-pound bag inside a giant Rubbermaid in the pantry.

"Where's Uncle Ben when you need him?"

"Uncle who?" She put the rice in the pot and started to rinse it off, three times.

"Never mind," I said.

She put the pot on the stove then made us coffee. We sat and talked in the kitchen. She told me about learning to cook from her father, and how he got up early to pack his lunch pail for work at the plantation. She told me about watching him chopping vegetables and cutting fish, and how he fixed his drill with a special blade to grate coconuts in their shells. She told me about Christmases at everybody's house.

When the water disappeared, she served the rice in little bowls with a shake of something mysterious from a spice jar, flecks of green and sesame seeds. *"Furikake,"* she said. It was good.

She gave me the pot and sent me home. "Try," she said. "Let me know."

It took days. Days of brown scum scraped off the bottom of the pot. Days of boiled over scales of dandruff on the burners. The rice god eluded me. He hid in the pot and stayed hard and crunchy and refused to cooperate. But I never gave up on him. I cooked him everyday and talked to him and pleaded the sincerity of my mission. Finally, one day he relented.

I waited patiently for the water to disappear, then lifted the lid off a pot of steamy, sticky, fragrant, translucent, perfect white rice. He was mine. And I was taking him to potluck.

My friend waited until then to give me another present, an electric aluminum pot with a black lid knob. "Now you can use the rice cooker," she said. "Save time. Just press the button."

"Wait a minute." I said. "Why didn't you give this to me in the first place? Why did you put me through all that?"

She smiled. The potluck culture must be deeper than I imagined. Perhaps it was enlightenment. Perhaps it was just part of the initiation. I felt like the Karate Kid. Rice on. Rice off.

As soon as they scheduled the next potluck, I called Christine.

"You gotta help me," I said. "I signed up for main dish."

Christine was delighted. "Chicken *hekka*," she said. "You're ready for it."

"I don't know," I said.

"It's easy. Get a pen."

"Are you sure? I was thinking of something like stew."

"You just get a bag of chicken thighs. Everything else is cans. Do you like mushrooms? We like ours with lots of mushrooms. You just cook the chicken a little bit first, then throw everything in the pot one time. Put the long rice in last. Don't forget to soak it first."

"How long do you have to soak it?"

"A few minutes. Whatever it says on the package."

"Then what?"

"Just throw it in at the last minute."

"The last minute before I go to bed, or the last minute before I leave the house in the morning, or the last minute before I serve it the next day?"

"Whatever you like."

"How do I know what I like? This is alien to me."

"Stop worrying. I'll come over and walk you through it the night before."

She gave me a long list of ingredients, checked to see if I had the right container, and told me to make sure somebody was bringing rice.

Potluck day was Tuesday. I picked up all the groceries on Sunday afternoon. On Monday night, I lined up the cans along the kitchen counter, rinsed out the crock pot and made coffee.

Christine called on her cellphone. "I'm still at Costco," she said. "I won't be back for a couple hours. Can you get started on your own?"

My heart sank. I looked at the cans of odd mushrooms and baby corn, the little packages of long rice with instructions in Japanese. "Oh sure," I said.

"Call if you need me to pick up something."

"I might need some paper plates."

She laughed. "Good luck!"

Here goes, I thought. At least I can cook the chicken. While the frozen chicken thighs slid around in the frying pan, I found a couple of recipes for *hekka* in the cookbook collection. They pretty much agreed on Christine's basic formula, with some variation in the amount of mushrooms and seasonings. One of them said to soak the long rice five minutes, in English. Thank God.

Somewhere along the way, between grating ginger and adding just a little more sesame oil, between leaving out the salt and adding sliced round onion (which wasn't in any of the recipes) I realized my chicken *hekka* was good. *My* chicken hekka.

We ate tuna sandwiches for dinner, while my creation stewed in the crockpot. I reassured my husband there would be plenty left over for dinner tomorrow night, not to worry. After the news, I put the crockpot in the refrigerator. I set our alarm clock for five o'clock so I could start warming it up before I went to work, and do the thing with the long rice.

That night I had a crazy dream—snorkeling around in a swampy stew of *hekka*, looking at all the ingredients and thinking how interesting they were—mushrooms, ginger, baby corn. Christine swam up and told me that round onion was a great addition. She was proud of me. Then suddenly a gooey school of long rice slithered all around us, threatening with their tentacles. Christine dug out; I was all alone. The long rice monsters were yelling at me. "You didn't soak us long enough! You threw us in too soon. We're going to ruin everything."

I don't remember if I woke up laughing or sweating. I do remember that the dish was a success. Nobody could believe it, especially me, when the general manager said "This tastes like it was cooked by a little old Japanese lady from Hilo."

Everyone congratulated me. I couldn't have been prouder.

Christine had not abandoned me, rather she pushed me out of the airplane like a sky-diving coach, and my parachute opened just fine.

I took home an empty crockpot.

That summer I went to the mainland on vacation. My family was astonished by my weight. They asked what you eat in Hawai'i, and to my own surprise I told them I'd make *lū'au* for everybody. This was easier said than done.

I had to order pork butts from the A&P because they didn't have any in the store. I searched the Oriental food sections of all the supermarkets until I found some *nori* and pickled ginger. I bought a rolling mat and chopsticks and a bag of rice. I drove out to Ethridge farm for raw peanuts to boil. I found Spam and pineapples at Safeway. There were no *lū'au* plates anywhere.

I started digging in my mother's backyard but she refused to let me bury the meat there. So I had to buy Liquid Smoke and use the turkey roasting pan instead. For two days her kitchen smelled burnt; everybody complained and opened the windows.

Taro was out of the question, so I improvised some *poi* from sweet potatoes in the blender. I couldn't find coconut cream anywhere, so I made chicken *lū'au* with frozen spinach and Coco Lopez frozen concentrate for Pina Coladas. I made macaroni salad with lots of mayonnaise, Portuguese bean soup with ham hocks and blackeyed peas, and the crazy Jell-O with six different layers and cream cheese in the middle. Of course there was no raw fish you could eat, and nothing even close to *'opihi*. So we bought crabs and steamed them up with Old Bay spice blend and *shoyu* and pretended it was *poke*. My mother had the perfect pot for rice.

When *lū'au* day came, we put beer in the coolers and set plastic chairs on the lawn. My niece made little cards for all the dishes with the names in English and Hawaiian, and we sewed *lei* out of honeysuckle. We dug out all the Christmas gifts I'd sent—Mom's monkeypod bowls and her *mu'umu'u*, my niece's grass skirt and coconut bra, the tropical tablecloths. We set out all the food, put on a Brothers Cazimero tape and stood back. It was a spread worthy of Uncle Billy's Sunday Brunch Buffet, $8.95.

Nobody ate.

They tried, they tasted. They wanted to know how everything was made. Nobody had ever seen anybody cook real rice before. The kids enjoyed the Jell-O. My brother said he wanted to learn how to roll *sushi*, so I gave him the mat and the leftover *nori*. My nephew liked slurping the *poi* off his fingers. My sister-in-law got hives all around her mouth from the pineapple. Her father said he'd eaten chicken and coconut in Thailand during the war. My other brother said it would've been better with collard greens. But everybody had a wonderful time, and the *lū'au* was considered a success.

The next day my mother made barbecue from the leftover *kālua* pig. And before I left they put together a care package for me to take home. A whole country ham. Ten pounds of raw peanuts. Homemade apple butter and strawberry preserves. Cans of Old Bay, blackeyed peas and collard greens.

Potluck culture to go. You carry something from Hawai'i to Virginia and from there to here. You bring together different ingredients for special occasions that different people celebrate. And what you end up with is better than what you started with.

I threw in a box of Uncle Ben's rice for Christine.

Because she's right. It isn't about the food. Potluck. First you have to have the right pot, the right attitude.

You bring what you have to the table. People eat it or they don't. Sometimes you have to improvise. You sign up for main dish and end up with a dessert. You don't know what all of the food is, but if you try everything you always find something to eat. You ask everybody how to make everything, and you say their food is good no matter what. And you always make a plate to take home. You eat together. You enjoy the meal. You share. You help clean up. And if your dish didn't turn out the way you thought it would, don't worry, you always get another chance.

And you can always bring paper plates.

PRINCESS CHICKEN HEKKA

3 lbs	Chicken thighs
1 can	Baby corn
1 can	Straw mushrooms
1 can	Button mushrooms
1 can	Bamboo shoots, sliced
1 can	Beer
1	Large onion, sliced
1	Thumb-size piece of ginger, peeled and sliced thick
Some	Garlic
4 pkg	Long rice
	Brown sugar and shoyu to taste
2-3	Green onions

Brown chicken with the round onion, ginger and garlic, then transfer to crock pot with remaining ingredients (except long rice). Stew at least two hours the night before your potluck. Just before time to leave soak long rice a few minutes (see package directions), then stir into crock pot and garnish top with chopped green onion. Serve with rice.

THE PET SITUATION

"There are pet people and there are non-pet people.

Non-pet people think people who keep animals in their houses are sick. Pet people usually *are* sick, with a pharmacopoeia of chronic problems including gastrointestinal distress caused by sharing bathrooms and/or kitchens with Kitty Clumpies, and anaphylactic reactions to pet hair, pet hair dander, the flea on the dander on the hair on the pet, the spray on the flea on the dander on the hair on the pet on the chair on the rug on the floor on the . . .

You get the picture. Not to mention bites and scratches.

The most common American pet people are cat and dog people. My husband and I fall into a lesser-known sub-category. We have birds. We have three blue and gold macaws to be precise, and that brings us to the beginning of the story. Almost.

It is first necessary to give the reader a little insight on a few of the basic differences between dogs and cats, and birds.

Dogs and cats are mammals. This means they are born live from their mothers.

Mother birds dump their babies before they are half-done and let them fight their way out of the shell all by themselves.

Dogs and cats are nourished at their mother's teats, snuggled up against her furry underbelly with warmth that inspires Hallmark cards and worldwide long-distance-call commercials.

Mother birds regurgitate half-digested food into the baby bird's mouth. This is accompanied by a lot of gagging and head bobbing on the part of the mother and desperate, half-crazed fluttering and screeching on the part of the young.

Another difference between dogs and cats and birds is their appearance as newborns. Puppies and kittens are little adorable-nesses that invariably elicit the "aw" reaction in both male and female humans.

A newborn blue and gold macaw—whose parents belong to a flock of magnificent rainbow fragments when soaring in flight above the Amazon jungles—resembles nothing so much as a sack of scrotum.

Make that a sack of spiny scrotum that says "ack" a lot, with eye buds and little flippers.

This appearance invariably enacts the "eeew" reaction in females and the "whoa" reaction in males, although it may well be Mother Nature's way of inducing the maternal feeding behavior described above.

All species display affection. Dogs wag their tails. Cats purr.

Birds re-enact the maternal feeding behavior. They throw up on you.

Personally, as a mammal, I think I'd rather put up with morning sickness than have to throw up on my baby's face every two hours. However, I do think there are advantages to laying an egg, as opposed to nine months of pregnancy inside your actual body. Birds may have a better system in that regard.

I've also read that in some species, the male does the actual egg sitting.

"Honey, it's halftime and I've got to take a leak. Can't you sit on this damn egg for a couple minutes? Honey? Couldn't she at least bring me another beer before she flies off?"

One thing birds do have in common with cats and dogs is that when injured they lick their wounds and are genetically incapable of stopping. And this finally brings us to the beginning of the story.

Last Tuesday, I went to get my husband and myself a second sunset beer, when I noticed that either a tiny axe murderer had sneaked into the birdcage, or else we had what pet people call a "Situation."

There was blood everywhere. It spattered the wall behind the birdcage, the perches inside, and most of the birds themselves. I couldn't tell which one was currently bleeding, or whether the blood was the result of some misguided human finger that had long since been consumed.

I went back downstairs with our beers. "Let me see your hands," I said to my husband. He held them up. Ten fingers. "We have a 'Situation,'" I said.

Up we go to investigate. We identify the victim and determine the source of the bleeding is one broken toenail. The bird does not seem upset by his injury and is contentedly licking his wound (see above) while the other two exercise their vocabulary in order to facilitate the investigation.

"Pistachios," they say. "Hello. Yum yum yum yum." They are quite explicit. "Pistachios."

This is a big help.

We decide to isolate the patient. We open the door to the cage, whereupon all three immediately exit and assume defensive positions out of reach. After bribery with pistachio nuts and some threat of physical violence, in English, we negotiate the injured bird onto a stick and into the bathroom, leaving the other two happily munching the doorframe.

"Do we have a styptic pencil?" asks my husband.

"Of course," I say. I open the first aid drawer, which consists of a quarter tube of Neosporin and half a box of Band Aids (see bites and scratches, above), a package of Benadryl (see anaphylactic reactions, above) and some tiger balm. I have no idea what that's for. "No, we don't," I say. "Do you want to try some flour?"

"Yes," says my husband with authority. "He's bleeding out."

I think we're watching way too much *ER*.

"Shall I order a CT, chem-7, head scan and portable chest film?"

He does not see the humor in this.

"Just the flour, I'm trying to get him stable."

The bird is a complicated little body. In order to stabilize one, it is necessary to drop a bath towel over its head, grab it by the wings and flip it on to its back. Then with your free hand (this would be your third hand if you happen to have one, otherwise you borrow one of your spouse's) grab the sucker's head by his jaw and hold firmly so that the beak does not encounter any fingers, thus rendering everyone helpless to everyone else.

We should note that blood now trails from the living room, across the bedroom carpet, bathroom tiles and a significant portion of our jeans and T-shirts, not to mention the above-mentioned towels.

I pause to wonder how much blood a bird actually contains. I have cut up whole chickens, but must assume that they have already "bled out" (see above) or else we don't have that much more to go.

The flour, which stays dusted on the broken toenail only for twelve nanoseconds before he licks it, is turning into an interesting pink batter, which splatters the surfaces not already spattered with the red stuff, with the exception of the one toenail.

Noting the procedure is ineffective, I volunteer to go to the store for a styptic pencil. My husband agrees. I give him the bird and I go.

At this point I have to report that either the majority of American males, pet or non-pet, have become significantly more careful with razors over the last 15 years, or else are in unanimous denial of the fact that they cut themselves while shaving. Stores, apparently, no longer see the need to carry the styptic pencil in their inventories. Men must be using flour to glue those little squares of toilet paper on their faces.

Returning empty handed, I page the veterinarian, and call a friend named Bob. If anyone would have a styptic pencil, he would. He offers to deliver, in exchange for a beer and pistachios.

The vet calls back: "Haven't you got a styptic pencil?" When I confess we don't, she says "Well, it's either that or electro-cauterization." I think she may be watching too much *ER*, too.

When Bob arrives, we stabilize him a with beer and attempt to apply the styptic onto the bird toe, whereupon we learn that the basic ingredient of this common household first aid product is, apparently, PVC plastic. Not only does it not "dissolve easily when moistened," no amount of grating, filing, chopping or chewing up and regurgitating will loosen up a molecule of the stuff. And, unlike a shaving injury, where one daubs it onto damp skin, followed by the little toilet paper squares, this is a hard, squirming surface to which nothing adheres and whose owner is losing his patience as rapidly as his blood.

We revert to the flour method. My husband brings in a half a pound in a paper towel, dredges the foot in same, flips me the bird and starts to leave. The bathroom takes on a snow-globe effect that makes me sneeze. (See anaphylactic, above)

"Wib you brig me by inhaler?" I ask.

"Sure," he says. "Keep it elevated." He goes to page the veterinarian again.

"Keeb wad elebaded?" I ask, lifting the bird foot, and my nose, just to be safe.

He doesn't come back for a while. I hear the phone ring and assume it's the vet calling back. I look at my little bird bundle, and I can't help thinking about my Uncle Petey in Arkansas, who used to love deep-fried chicken feet with ketchup. Eeew.

I take him into the kitchen to get the inhaler and some air, and to check on the progress of the prognosis. I hear my husband explaining to the vet how, yes, his arc-welding rig could get hot enough to do an electric cauterization, but it might not be the best thing for the bird. The other two have devoured two-thirds of the doorframe and are working on the entertainment center.

"How's it going?" says Bob.

"Nod do good," I say.

I get the inhaler and go back and sit on the toilet with the bird upside down in my lap. My eyes are watering; my nose is dripping; I'm trying to stifle sneezes so as not to startle the patient. As if he understands that I'm trying to help, the bird lets me pet him. This is a breakthrough, since birds, as a species, barely tolerate me. Soon he's making little *ack* noises and the bleeding stops enough so he can roll over onto his feet. He very gently takes my fingers and shows me where he wants attention —behind his head, under his wings, on the side of his cheek patches. We are bonding.

Then to my horror he starts to bob his head and gag. What emerge from his craw are three greenish, bloody pebbly things that bounce on the new pizza decor of my bathroom floor. In a panic I snatch him back up, grab what's left of the floured paper towel, scoop up what I believe are my poor baby's innards, and dash into the kitchen where my husband is still talking to the vet on the phone, now about using the propane torch, and how it might not set fire to the patient.

"He just coughed these up," I say, smacking them into his hand like a surgical nurse. He examines them carefully. I take the patient back into isolation to prepare for the worst. In a moment my husband comes in, looking serious, still holding wrapped-up bird guts.

"The Doctor said not to worry about those things," he says.

"What are you talking about?" I say.

"You were petting him, so he fed you."

"Oh my God. What are they?"

"Pistachios. "

"Eeew."

"They're only bloody because he was licking his toe."

"You mean he's going to be OK?"

"Yes, hon," he says gently, handing me the paper towel back, "He is."

Full of relief and affection, and overwhelmed with pride for him and for the way we've dealt with our pet "Situation" together, I do what most comes naturally at a special moment like this.

I throw up on his feet.

ORANGES FROM EGYPT

"Where will you be buried, Kits?" There was a pause, and I wondered if she heard me. She was studying the Big Island through the car window as we drove from Waikōloa down Queen K highway through Kona and farther south. The road was long and straight, carved into Pele's black sculptures, bordered by white rock messages and the bright ocean beyond.

Kits, my husband's father's sister, had been a Sister of the Holy Cross in Dhaka, Bangladesh for fifty years. To honor her fiftieth anniversary, the Community gave her a vacation following the requisite trip to their home base in Indiana. After her month there, she chose to visit us in Hawai'i, before the long flight through Tokyo and Thailand back to Bangladesh.

Today she opted to see the City of Refuge instead of the volcano, since I told her they were too far apart to do both. We put on our jeans and sunglasses and took the camera to Pu'u Honua O Hōnaunau.

"I'm sorry, that's a weird question," I said.

"Not at all," she said, as steadily and clearly as she had said everything. "There is a place for us outside of the university in Dhaka. Several of our sisters are there, and a Maryknoll priest who actually died of rabies in 1962. He refused the treatments, for some reason. The Brothers weren't able to convince him and we never understood why."

Rabies. I'm afraid of dogs.

"He was such a strong and vibrant man, such a value to the community. In the hospital, they were only able to make him comfortable, to suppress his . . . delirium." She turned back to the window. "It wouldn't make sense to go to all the expense of sending us back to the United States. I will be buried at the place where I have spent the majority of my life."

Kits started as a nurse, but once they had trained enough local nurses to care for the sick, she taught anthropology at the university in Dhaka, which the community also built. Education was allowed to be more of a priority when people's health was less of a crisis.

As I listened, I thought, *You've done enough for two lives. At least. I'm so jealous. I'm so jealous of your accomplishments and your travel stories. How can you be a nun and a nurse and a doctor of anthropology all at once—when I can just barely get through typing and filing and answering the phone? How can you be so intelligent and interested in everything? How can you have developed opinions on world issues—when I can just barely remember the end of ER from week to week?*

"I've pretty much decided to be cremated," I said. "But I don't know what to do with the ashes."

"The Hindu cremate their dead," she began. "The Christians and Moslems bury, and the funerals take place very quickly because there's no refrigeration. There's no time for anyone to travel if they hear of a death in the family. Land is at such a premium though, that they've begun to bury them on top of existing graves. During the monsoon and then the flood season, we have had serious problems with the coffins floating up. The government may have to make a bigger case for cremation."

Please don't ask what Hawaiians traditionally do because I don't know. I know that they hid the bones of the ali'i, and I know that they made fish hooks out of their enemies' bones, but I don't know what the average family did. You would know by now if you lived here. You would be speaking the language by now.

She told a story about an English couple which was visiting the embassy when the husband died of a heart attack. The Sisters had to keep his body in the school's refrigerator because it was the only one large enough, while they arranged flights to England. Somehow when the body arrived without a death certificate, it had to be sent back to Dhaka and then back to England again.

That's a long trip to your grave.

We have passed by Kailua town and the Little Grass Shack in Kealakekua. "Those are coffee trees," I told her.

"Oh, where?" She was genuinely excited. We pulled over and I picked her a sprig of the red cherries, certain the farmer wouldn't mind. "I would never have thought it would be such a beautiful plant. And how do they get the coffee from this?"

This I could at least talk about, and I told her what I knew of picking and drying, the little work-donkeys, the Kona nightingales, hauling loads of cherries down the mountain trails. As we drove past coffee towns, hung high above the ocean, we could smell the heavenly aroma of coffee beans in old-fashioned brass roasters. "There's an old factory down there somewhere, with a shop and stuff." We decided to stop for a cup and made the turn *makai*, down the endless twisting road toward the coast. It was a perfectly clear day. You could see Captain Cook's monument.

"What are those trees there, with the long sticks of red flowers?" she asked.

I managed the curve and looked back in the mirror. One tire skipped onto the shoulder.

"They call it umbrella tree. It's something like schefflera."

"I'm sorry. I shouldn't ask you to look while you're driving."

"Did I scare you?"

"No," she laughed, "but it's not fair for me to keep saying 'look' and you can't look. But there's so much to look at. Is that a mongoose?"

"Yes." He made it across the road in front of us, and I slowed down a little. "Those are papaya trees. Do you have papayas in Bangladesh?"

"Yes, we do, but they're bigger I think. And bananas, and we eat a lot of things with coconut. But you know, a real treat for us is when someone brings us oranges from Egypt or other kinds of fruit. It's surprising what a treat an orange can be."

"It must be hard—to miss having so many things."

"Oh no. We don't miss things any more. At first you do. And my mother used to send me things like—oh, hand lotion and things like that. But after a while you get over all that. Then things, surprises, are just wonderfully special."

Mental note: Buy oranges.

At the bottom of the hill, but before the coffee factory, I saw the historical marker on the left side of the road: Painted Church. "I want to take you here," I said, turning off. "My mother said I had to show you this."

"Your mother did? Did you bring her here?"

"Yes, when she and my sister came to see us."

"Is your mother still alive?"

"Yes."

I then realized we came the wrong way, or at least the long way. We were facing miles of a one-lane road through remote house lots, fronted by children and dogs who seemed suspicious of our presence. I stopped at a washout to let a huge truck pass. It looked menacing, and the tinted windows prevented us from seeing people inside. Kits was talking about her mother, about when she decided to enter the convent.

How does she do it? How does she remember so clearly and express herself so well? Is it living your whole life without men or money? Does that free up so much space in your brain that you can actually think like this?

She was saying, "And when my mother died, I thought: 'Now there's nothing left between me and eternity, between me and God.'"

I can hear the capital G in God.

On the right, the *makai* side, an old woman with a face like a crumpled paper bag was picking up her newspaper from the plastic box at the end of her drive. Her little white poi dog yapped at her worn-flat slippers. She lifted a hand as we approached.

In greeting? Do I know her?

I slowed down to see her better and a red rental car came barreling towards us in the middle of the road, paying no attention. I jerked the wheel, put on the brakes and slid a little in the gravel, knocked into the paper box and leaned it over. The rental car breezed by. The old woman was already halfway down the driveway, heading for her house.

Where is the damn dog?

I got out of the car and luckily the post was not broken. I was able to straighten it back up with a rock. Nobody came up the drive, no huge sons or flocks of grandchildren. No dogs.

"Are you OK?" I called towards the house. "I'm sorry about the box, but it's fixed now!" Kits wisely stayed in the car. As I got in she pointed to a marker on the *mauka* side of the road—the second turnoff for the church. I had forgotten about it. I pulled back onto the road warily, looking for the little white dog, but he was nowhere in sight.

"That was a little exciting," I said to Kits as we executed a new series of narrower curves and turns.

"It's lucky you're such a good driver," she said calmly.

Finally we reached St. Benedict's Painted Church perched on the hill, at peace. We drove past Our Lady of Hawai'i painted on a wooden plank mounted in the *ti* leaf garden, and parked in the shade. There was no one around.

"Look at the graveyard," she said excitedly, climbing out of the car. "Look at how beautiful, and you can see the ocean. Do you think we can go in?"

A stone path, planted all along with orchids and heliconia, led past a coconut-thatched souvenir stand. Postcards and Christmas ornaments were laid out for sale on the honor system. The brass cash box looked as old as the church, "est. 1899." In front, spread out like picnics, were the graves. They were decorated with pots of flowers and growing plants, some with *lei*, some with paper windmills, some with incense and candles.

It is a remarkable graveyard. You could film "Our Town" in this graveyard, and all the dead would sit there in the sunshine watching their families fish and farm, talking over the comings and goings, talking over the living and the life to come.

"Look how beautiful," she said again. "Are those orchids? And what are those big red flowers?"

"Anthuriums," I told her. "*Obake.*"

"Look—the cemetery goes all the way up the hill past the church. Do you think we can go inside the gate?"

What could it hurt? A chain link fence enclosed the graveyard, with an entrance part way down the hill. There was a padlock, but it was open. I offered my hand and she deferred, using the fence for balance. Inside she walked, smiling, up and down the rows as if visiting, as if admiring works of art. The sun was bright and I worried about her in the heat.

An ocean breeze lifted her short hair as she stooped to read a name or a date on a headstone. She looked up the long hill. A dog was barking up there in the trees, and to me it sounded like the same yak yak yak of the little white mutt at the paper box.

Well at least I didn't run over him. But that was far from here, wasn't it? Maybe not. It's a pretty crooked road. Come on, Kits. It's hot out here. Don't you want to go inside? What is it with the graveyard and all this talk about the dead? Is our irony catching up with us? Do you need some water? Should I have brought sunblock? If anything happens way out here what will we do? Why doesn't that dog shut up?

"OK," she said, rubbing her hands on her jeans. "Let's look at the church." We made our way up the *pu'u* and were greeted by a bust of Father Damien. He was a familiar figure to Kits, who knew all about his work on Moloka'i, all about his beatification, all about Hansen's disease. The bust was set in the shade, draped with a *ti* leaf *lei*, and seemed to oversee the graveyard from under the broad brim of his hat. I took a picture of the two of them, then she patted him on the shoulder and we went inside.

The Painted Church is an exuberant celebration of God. A fiery hell burns on one wall, and on the other, dramas of the Bible. Cain slays Abel. Christ rejects the Devil. Scenes of passion and violence from a missionary's nightmares play out in vibrant colors, belied by the little church's calm white facade. An ancient spiral staircase leads up to what must be the choir loft, supported by barber-pole pillars with an explosion of palm fronds painted at the top. The ceiling is a study of white clouds in a lapis Kona sky. Glorious angels guard the altar. Everywhere there are flowers from the gardens—the orchids and anthuriums, *ti* leaf. The angels are smiling and warmly welcoming.

Kits walked straight up the aisle to the altar.

I am not going to be surprised if she ascends into Heaven right before my eyes. I am going to stand right here and if a miracle is going to hap-

pen today, I am not going to let it scare me. I am going to get a picture.

Then, without any special effects whatsoever she turned and walked out, past me and my camera. I followed.

Outside, she looked over at the rectory. "There is no car in the garage," she said, a little disappointed. "I would've liked to meet the priest."

We looked in the backyard. There, sitting all alone in the green grass was a steeple.

"It must be St. Benedict's previous one," she said. "They must be saving it for something. Although I don't know what one does with a used steeple."

Unless there's a church buried underneath. It looked very strange to me and I wanted to move on.

Then, I remembered something else that I wanted to show her—uphill of the church, in the garden. I looked past the spare spire and spotted the rocky trail, shaded on one side with iron-woods and a brilliant red blooming hedge on the other. We headed up. The trail was marked every eight feet or so with a rustic wooden cross, each carved with a number.

"Oh my. It's the Stations of the Cross," she said.

"Yes," I said, "and these bushes are crown of thorns, all along here. And look." I pointed up to the very top, where sat, unbelievably, its perfect white marble luminous in the sunlight, the Pietà. Mary held her son's lifeless body as she might have held his infant body, so that he could see all the way to the ocean, all the way to the ends of his creation. In this beautiful place even Mary's grief was calmed.

"Oh my glory," said Kits. "This we have to do. I need a picture of this for our sisters. The Pietà is a very special symbol for us. It is something we have brought with us from the very beginning, and our Bangladeshi sisters love this statue so much. They have all lost so much. It is very close to their hearts."

I offered my hand for the steep little hike and this time she took it. Her hand was smooth and youthful, not at all marked by the hard work it had done. She walked deliberately, using me only for balance on the uneven footing.

She's almost a foot taller than me. I couldn't stop her if she did start to fall. She must have been imposing in the old days, in her big black habit, marching up and down the hills of Bangladesh. Do they have hills in Bangladesh? Well, up and down the school halls and hospital corridors, then.

We took our time going up. She told another story about seeing Michelangelo's Pietà in Rome and the Pope and what a magnificent trip it was. She was wondering how in the world they brought this huge statue all the way here and placed it and who would have thought and so forth. She was telling me that Pietà means pity, and that the impossible grace of the statue is engineered to evoke pity for the Virgin, for any woman who has lost her child.

"Look at that," she said, approaching it. "See how easily she holds Him? Can you imagine having a full-grown man draped across your lap like that? Can you imagine how strong you would have to be?"

She removed her sunglasses and smiled at the camera and me. I clicked away, moving around her, wishing I could photograph the real look of her face. It, like the statue, had this quality of lightness—as in weightlessness, as in radiance—yet based so sturdily on the earth.

The chances of this photograph coming out are so remote I don't even want to think about it. I hope they have a postcard of the statue back down at the shack. I hate to have responsibility for other people's important moments. It's not fair. Just because we live here and this is their once-in-a-lifetime trip.

"Thank you so much for bringing me here," she said when we

reached the top. "This is extraordinary." I took the picture. I hoped for the best.

Later, sipping one hundred percent Kona peaberry and eating avocado sandwiches at the coffee factory, she asked how far it was to the volcano from here. "About ninety miles," I said.

"Oh, that's very far."

At the door, Auntie Bess was in her chair, smiling and saying hello to the people as they came in, directing them to the movie room with her coffee-wood cane. Her little white dog padded back and forth nervously behind the counter. Two enormous cats slept across the glass display cases, ignoring all activity.

You want to go for it don't you? Anthropology is one thing, but creation happening right in front of you is something else again. I'm not tired yet. Something about being with you is . . . what? Empowering. If you, at seventy, having seen everything, having come all this way and having all that way to go—well the least I can do is show you. We will go all the way around. You will keep talking to me and I will not get tired and this will be an adventure we will neither one forget.

"You want to go for it, don't you?"

Her eyes flashed at me. Yes she did. We debated two or three minutes about the fact that it would be such a long way for me to drive and she didn't want to impose. Then we called my husband to let him know we'd be late. Amazed that we were going all the way around the island, he told us to have a good time and drive carefully.

Since we had come so far, we stopped for a cursory walk-through and said a brief hello to the gathering of *tiki* at Pu'u Honua o Hōnaunau, then we headed south again. She told me stories, and we asked each other questions. The weather was decent and the drive was easy through South Kona, through the forest preserve.

"I'm so surprised to find that you're happy here," she said.

"Did you think we wouldn't be? We've been here seven years."

"No, that's not exactly what I meant. Has it been seven years already? I just meant that this is so different from where you two came from. It has to be lonely. Don't you miss your family and your friends?"

"You did the same thing, Kits," I said, laughing. She laughed too. "I've found that it's easy to pick up where you leave off with people."

"I guess so," she agreed. She started another story—about a fellow nurse she met on a train trip through India. It was during wartime, and they were being evacuated from the villages to hospitals in safer places. It was dangerous, but they thought of it as an adventure. They remained friends, visited when they could, and wrote letters. Many years later, they ran into each other in England and spent a whole night walking up and down the beach, talking.

I believe that, easily.

We had rounded the very bottom of the island and had started north, gradually up the Hilo side.

We were passing by Mark Twain's monkeypod trees in Na'alehu town.

"Oh, yes," she said with certainty, "friendship spans time and distance. There's no question."

Beyond Na'alehu no one was on the road and I was cruising along fast. We had a long way to go.

"You know, I can remember the first time I ever saw a nun," I said.

"You can?"

"Uh huh, I was just a little girl, and for some reason my father went grocery shopping instead of my mother. He took me along. The first thing that happened was I nearly fell out of the car. I can remember watching the big tire go around while I'm hanging out the door with him holding on to my foot for dear life. Then inside the store, I see this, looked like to me, huge woman in her big black dress and I remember yelling, 'Look, Daddy, a witch, a witch, a witch!'"

"Your poor father," she said, laughing.

"He never took me to the store again."

"Are those *nēnē*?" she asked suddenly, leaning to look over me.

"Where?" I looked up in the hills where she was pointing. "No those are regular gee . . ."

Yak Yak Yak Yak. *Oh my god it's a dog in the road. Slam on the brakes. Steer with the skid. Where did he go? Did we hit him? Straighten out. Pull off to the right. Where is he?*

"He must've run off in the brush," I said to Kits as she climbed out of the car. "There's nothing under the car and there's no blood or anything. We must've missed him." I looked under the car, back behind us, in the brush on the side of the road. "We must've missed him," I said again.

Damn dogs.

"Are you all right? Kits?"

She stood, transfixed, looking ahead. Far in the distance was the towering column of steam that marked where living lava entered the ocean. It was hundreds of feet tall, an enormous finger from heaven holding the place where the four elements—earth, air, fire and water—all came together.

"This is impossible. We've got to be thirty miles away," I said. She didn't seem to think it was impossible.

She doesn't seem to think anything is impossible.

We continued our adventure. When we reached Volcanoes National Park it was raining. The Rangers at the Visitors Center told us the road was closed near the eruption site because of the weather. "Too much steam. You can't get close to the lava. " They smiled and said that Madame had closed the show for today.

We know better, don't we? We know she has given us a rare treat, in each other, today.

"Oh, I don't see how anything could be more magnificent than what we already witnessed," she said, not at all disappointed. "Are there other things to do in the park?"

We headed out again, to Thurston Lava Tube, its trickling darkness soothing and serene after so many miles of sightseeing.

The underworld. This is a different painted church. This is the shadow of God.

When we came out, she wanted to see the nature trail, and it wasn't too muddy. We walked a while through the fern forest. She paused in the path, looking up into the trees.

"What are those, with the beautiful red flowers?" she asked.

"'Ōhi'a, lehua. It's one of Pele's . . . " I began.

"Shhh." So many birds were singing and chatting above us, as the day deepened into afternoon. I could actually see them, red honeycreepers and *'elepaio* and *what are those?* flickering in the high, living canopy.

Like tiny colorful angels. How did she spot them?

We doubled back, past the Art Center to what I called the "drive-in volcano." On the side of the road was a place where we could look into a permanent steam vent, chugging its little cloud out for visitors all day long. She practically jumped out of the car.

"It's so warm," she said, waving her hands in the mist, "How far down does the crack go?"

"All the way," I said.

"All the way," she repeated, peering over the rail, deep into the earth.

Is hell down there?

We continued around Crater Rim Drive to the observatory

and walked the short distance to the lookout where the primeval expanse of Halema'uma'u lies open before us, a ghostly coliseum of rock and steam.

A cluster of tourists was talking and taping each other with a lot of fuss as Kits moved patiently from one marker to the next. I dodged the video cam, trying to photograph her, studying, against the backdrop of the crater.

"Listen to this," she read. "There was an aboriginal temple on this point. It was called Uwēkahuna, 'The Place of Priestly Weeping.'"

"What?" I never heard this before. She showed me. I could not help but make the connection with the Pietà, and I felt the chicken skin response to the thought twinkle up my arms. I wondered if Kits felt it too.

Mary's grief, her physical strength and the sense of peace of the place. The sense of peace, the priests who weep, and Pele's power of procreation, also in stone.

We left the park in fading daylight and began the long drive, stopping in Hilo for gas and a 7-Eleven coffee. From there we cruised around the Hāmākua coastline, and through Waimea to Waikōloa.

"A cold beer is going to taste pretty good when we get home," I said. She agreed, and told me about going to the American Club in Dhaka to drink a glass of beer with one of her friends. "It is an adventure in itself just to get across the city. You either take the local bus or sampan-taxi. It's too dangerous to walk because the traffic is so bad."

Bangladesh. How can you live in a place like that? Where pollution, traffic and crime have a stranglehold, where horrific poverty is no longer frightening but commonplace, where it sounds like every known plague and every catastrophe of nature visit on a regular basis. How can you live there and be so much at peace?

"I don't even wear this crucifix when I go out. One of our Sisters had hers stolen from around her neck in the middle of the afternoon."

"How do you stand it?" I had to ask. "Aren't you afraid all the time? Between the criminals and the diseases and all the awful things?"

"Oh no, " she said. "It's our home. They know us. And it's not like the people are suffering all the time. Only when you have nothing, the smallest things have value."

Yes, the smallest things. Like doctorates and languages. Like meeting Mother Teresa.

"Like friends. Like a visit to the American Club. A trip to a beautiful place."

"Did you always want to be a nun?"

"Oh, yes. I knew from—" She lifted her graceful hand to show a little child, then taller and taller. "I always knew."

"Do you think everybody has a mission, like that?" I asked.

"God has a plan for everybody," she said. "I believe that."

"It would make things so much easier if we knew what it was."

"Easier," she said patiently, "but without the surprises."

Like oranges from Egypt.

As we pulled in the driveway, my husband, her nephew, was waiting for us. He had set out the cooler and chairs and lit the *hibachi*.

"I thought you all might like a steak for dinner," he announced, handing us our cold beers as we climbed out of the car for the last time on this long day. The moon was rising over the roof. Somewhere down the hill, a little dog was barking, welcoming someone home.

During the second beer I asked my husband, "Where do you want to be buried?"

THE BARD OF HĀMĀKUA

In the back of the refrigerator in our house is a plain brown bottle of home-brewed beer. It doesn't have a label. It has been there since the last-Sunday-of-the-month cookout when its companions were consumed on the spot. An interesting drink, with tastes of honey and spices, yeast, and something vaguely green like lemon grass, it seemed to require a little too much thinking for a beer.

The bottle was brought to us by the Bard of Hāmākua.

The goddess awoke from her nap, stretched and yawned, causing a gust of wind to whip down the Kalapana coastline. Sightseeing helicopters bounced around for a moment like dragonflies passing a fan. She wiggled her toes and a 3.5 temblor registered on the machines at the Volcano Observatory.

"What shall I wear today?" She looked through her closet, considering the soft white fur of the dog coat, or the comfortable shoes and loose skin of the grandmother, or the hundred other forms she assumed. "I'm so bored," she said.

She swam in the sea and rinsed in a rainstorm, shaking her

long hair into a warm breeze to dry. She admired her nakedness in the sun and thought, *Not too bad for a middle-aged goddess.*

The last thousand years had treated her well, but such beauty was not meant to be alone. It was time to find someone to share it with, time for a man, a young man, who could show her a good time. She laughed toward the ocean and a pair of dolphins popped out of the water like champagne corks, slapped the surface with their tails and disappeared.

She turned and looked towards the mountain. *From atop Mauna Kea*, she thought, *I could see all the young men on the island.* "Yes," she said, and began her ascent.

The phone rang in the kitchen, as I was skewering vegetables and pieces of beef for the cookout. Cherry tomato, beef, onion, beef, green pepper, beef, mushroom.

"It's Bard," said the voice on the phone.

"Hey," said I, "Where are you?" One never knew. He had called from all of his adventures. He called from the bakery on Johnston Atoll, where he worked baking pies. He called from Oregon where he was logging with his uncle. On those calls he spoke loudly, his hearing less than normal after hours with the chain saw. He called from Maui where he was on a hunt for an old fire engine he wanted to buy and from Honolulu where he was searching for parts for an old Volvo. Once he called from a guy's house who wanted to get rid of some birds. Did we want a Catalina macaw or a young cockatoo? No, not this time, Bard.

"I'm on Saddle Road," he said. "With a German named Stein who wants to see the mountain. We're going to drive up to the summit in his rental car and then I'm going to bring him down the back way." He laughed. "It's a Neon."

"A Neon?" I asked.

"Yeah sure. I'll make it," he said.

"OK. If you say so."

"So we might be a little late but we're coming to the party tonight. OK?"

"Sure, Bard," I said.

"What can we bring?" he asked. He always asked.

"Just bring some stories, Bard," I told him, as usual. He always did.

"OK, see you."

Cherry tomato, beef, onion, beef. Bard was always creating another story. Of all the people who might show up tonight, he was one I could always count on to be entertaining. Everyone, from the babyless boomers like us to the neighbors with kids and their *tūtū*, everyone was a fan of Bard's stories and adventures.

He knew the hidden roads to get to the gates, to access the trails, to hike to the back of all the best waterfalls, all the most spectacular *pali* views of Hāmākua. And, whether his transportation was by foot, horseback, one of a long string of surviving Volvos or a rented Neon with a German named Stein, Bard could guarantee an adventure, and something you had never seen before. At twenty-six he knew more about the island than many people much older did. It must have started with small kid days, walking down the hill to school.

"One time I talked my friends into cutting through this pasture. I knew this bull—"

"We had a ditch that ran from the top of the hill all the way down to the ocean, and after a big rain, you could take one of those Styrofoam coolers and—"

"We found this cave, and you wouldn't believe the stuff—"

It went on. It was endless. At the last-Sunday-of-the-month

parties he would pace up and down, waving his arms and smoking Camels, regaling us with stories of his adventures, plans for his inventions, ideas for new ones of either.

He was so *haole*, so white. He was a pale, blue-eyed blond and too thin, as if he used up every drop of energy that went into his body, even though he ate like a local boy and could tell his stories in pidgin just as well. He fell into it naturally, the way you fall into pace with someone as you walk along a trail.

"Brah, you folks like come with us next Saturday? We go up Hi'ilawe the back way, brah, in my uncle's truck. He get all the keys to the gates inside there. We might stay camping or just talk story little while and come back *bumbye* a different way. You like go?"

Beef, cherry tomato, beef, green pepper. Once he had called from California, so in love with a woman named Helena. I was glad he had found someone who appreciated his special spirit. I was glad to hear he was having great sex. He had always seemed too busy to bother with that sort of thing before. He thought he could stay working at this restaurant, baking specialty breads, until he could make a deal with this friend of a friend who was going to open his own place. Then he, Bard, could concentrate on making some serious money with his latest enterprise, importing fish.

"What kind of fish?" I asked.

"*'Ahi, ono,*" he said, "anything from Hawai'i. Local fish will drive these California foodies crazy! You can't serve any kind of mainland fish without cooking it! Do you know what they'll pay for anything fresh from Hawai'i?" He always had a dream. "Then I'll be able to bring her and her little girl back home and we can buy a house up *mauka*; get started on what I really want to do."

"And what's that, Bard?" I asked.

"Water," he said. "Half the island's got nothing but rain and the other half's a desert. I'm going to buy this old fire engine and collect water from catchments and deliver it to the dry side. I'm renting the acreage from a friend of my grandmother's, and on the same land as the catchment system, we can grow mac nuts. Macadamia nuts are the next rage on the mainland. Kona coffee takes too much work and too much time. And somebody has managed to prove that macadamia nut oil actually reduces cholesterol in your body. Does all kind of good things for you. You wait. Then I'm going to make electricity and sell it to the county."

"How?"

"With this turbine I got from an old sugar factory. I can make enough electricity to light Hilo and still be able to build the Tesla coil."

"The what?'

"You know, Nikolai Tesla, the magic mad scientist?"

"No, not really."

"Compared to him, Thomas Edison was just a dim bulb."

"I see," I said. "What are you going to push the turbine with, Bard?"

"With steam from the water in the catchments," he explained. "Which I will heat with the bagasse and mac nut shells . . . as soon as I find a good used boiler."

I didn't want to ask where one finds a good used boiler. "How does she feel about the plan?" I asked, getting him back to the juicier subject of his ladylove.

"She doesn't want to come to Hawai'i."

"Has she ever been here?"

"No, not yet." He didn't want to talk about that little snag. He told me how wonderful she was again and how beautiful. He told me he was sure she would get used to the idea, because if he loved it so much, then how could she not?

Then my husband got on the phone and they talked for an hour about a new invention. He loved to run his inventions by

Dwight; they could talk forever about the potential of this, that or the other. This one, after a lengthy discussion about the impossibility of picking up a used boiler, was a smokeless cigarette which used a hi-tech filter to capture all the particulates in an enclosed tube after you exhaled into a mouthpiece.

Dwight asked for one of his engineering books and I brought it to him, then poured another cup of coffee and stopped trying to listen. The Bard in love. What a funny thought. All that creative energy could be romantic genius if converted into love.

It was a brilliantly sunny day, and the goddess took her time going up *mauka*. It was a long trip to the top of the mountain. She surveyed the lonely stretch of black lava that cut a line between the land and the ocean. To the south, barreling clouds of steam marked where the lava entered the water. As she rose higher, she could see her artwork in the older flows which painted the even older slump of land that fell a hundred feet down a hundred years ago. She remembered how the earthquake shook the island, then created a *tsunami* that washed the loose debris of human life off the coast and out to sea.

Above the palisades were the short *'ōhi'a* forests and cooler temperatures, a little mist, a little rain and giant ferns coiling like unanswered question marks from the unseen soil below. She wrapped a cloud around her body and permitted a patch of sunshine to fall between the mosaic of branches, where little bird gypsies sang, heard only by themselves and the goddess as she rose.

She continued upward, above the forests, above the clouds. Finally she was eye-to-eye with the summit, the *piko* of the mountain, and from there her goddess eyes could see the island in its entirety. She saw the petticoat of white sand beaches all around, pinned with their fancy resorts. She saw the overgrown sugar cane fields with their fences now and real estate signs. She saw the speculative subdivisions encroaching on the empty spaces like a different kind of lava flow. She saw the telescopes around her, forever gazing heavenward, forever looking for something. She saw a funny little turquoise car smoking and choking its way up the cinder road to the mountaintop.

"We're gonna make it!" said Bard. His foot mashed the pedal to the floor. "Wait'll we get to the top. You won't believe it."

"I don't really believe it now," said Stein.

Bard laughed out loud. He watched the gauges and kept them all in the safety range. Even though he believed in pushing things, he knew better than to risk that long walk back down the mountain. They were almost out of the overcast and drizzle. Soon the clouds would be below them and he'd get the rush he was waiting for. His heart pounded with excitement and thin air. He enjoyed bringing people up here. He loved to share that first gasp when they hit all that crystal blue sky and knew it was their first breath of the atmosphere of gods.

"Maybe nobody thinks it's as awesome as I do," said Bard. He liked to downplay the moment a bit, just before it hit. "I don't know. Tell me what you think, because I'm always interested in people's first—" The car passed the last of the clouds. He heard Stein's deep inhale.

"Wow."

Where was I? Beef, onion, beef, mushroom. Oh yes, it's the last Sunday of the month. The brown bottle is not in the refrigerator yet. Bard, the Bard of Hāmākua, was in love once. But like so many of the dreams in that eclectic brain, it had not worked out. His love for Hawai'i was too great and she couldn't handle the move. They would always be friends, he had said when he came back. They would always keep in touch.

At least this relationship had opened doors for him, it seemed. He talked with joy about his girlfriends now. He sometimes brought them to the house and they were always characters for some future story. One pretty, dark-haired girl seemed nice. She wanted to learn how to play the bass, and her favorite group was Black Sabbath. I laughed and told her I remembered Black Sabbath from my era.

"That's what we listen to," she said seriously. She put on a CD and played air guitar, actually bass, to it, while Bard beamed at her and drank too much. At the end of the night I had given her a B vitamin and told her to take his keys. She was nervous about driving the stick shift, but felt she could handle it even though she didn't have her license. I thought she meant with her. We found out later she was only fifteen. I could've killed him.

"Bard—she's only fifteen and you brought her to our house and we drank with her and then you got too drunk to drive and we made her take you home without a license!"

"It all worked out OK, didn't it?" he said, as he always did, and it always did. He said he was teaching her about the world for three years and then he was going to marry her. No sex. Not yet. He didn't want trouble with the law.

He liked to talk about women. He liked women very much.

"First, I find one of those mossy-toed girls from Puna," he told us once. "You know, the kind that never wear shoes, and never went anywhere or did anything. Then, I buy them the appropriate outfit to go out to dinner with me."

"Including shoes?" someone asked.

"Including shoes and everything else," he said.

"What kind of an outfit?"

"You know, nice skirt, kind of long and colorful and one of those lacy kind of blouses, with the ruffly things around here," he drew a line across his shoulders. "You know, peasant kind of thing." *Perfect for the Bard* I thought. "And then I take her to Paolo's. It's a wonderful Italian restaurant in Pāhoa. You wouldn't believe how good the food is. Paolo always treats me like a king! He says . . ." (At this point Bard assumes a broad Hawaiian-raised Italian accent.)

"He says, 'Bard-a, how good to see you again. Would you like to try the *veal piccata* tonight? Bene! But first, you must have *antipasti* and a glass of Chianti Classico!' And he sweeps us out the back door to this great little intimate table under the trees in back of the dining room. And he brings the wine and stands there talking to us while he rolls a smoke. I drink the wine and maybe have a cigar. And the violin player comes out to serenade us and that girl is taking all this in, not believing any of it. And she's toast! It's the most romantic thing in the world and she's digging it!"

"You're going to get in trouble, Bard," I said. "Seducing these little mossy-toed Puna girls."

"No sex!" he declared. "No sex, that's the key. I'm going to show them the world and then—" He always had a plan.

The goddess remembered her nakedness and dropped softly to the ground at the summit. She slipped behind one of the telescopes and put on her *'ōhi'ā* tree dress, placing its scarlet *lehua* flowers in her long hair, letting it blow in the wind. From there she watched the little car arrive at the top and its two occupants jump out into the cold thin air. Both were men, one with a husky build, the other long and lanky, with white-blond *haole* hair. The bigger one had a camera and was actively clicking it all around. He was amazed at the view, amazed at the mountain. He bounced around and talked loudly as people do when they are cold, saying, "Hoo, boy," and things like that.

The leaner one nodded, answering him. He pointed out things to photograph. "Look at that *'ōhi'a*," he said. "It's way too high for it to grow. It shouldn't be here." He walked over to her and touched the flower behind her ear, but he didn't pick it.

He knows the rules, she thought. She held her breath at his touch and trembled slightly, producing a little gust of even colder wind that made the men shiver in their flannel shirts and the bigger one with the camera jump back into the car.

"Let's go, Bard. You said it takes hours to get back down. Hoo, boy, it's cold." The blond one nodded and walked back to the car.

"Bard," the goddess whispered. He turned and looked briefly back at the tree, then got in the car and they started down. She followed, out of sight as the Neon bounced and jostled and coughed through clouds of dust for the next two hours. She waved a hand and cleared the more threatening rocks from the treacherous road, she listening to his stories; she was fascinated. How could one so young have learned her island and its secrets so well?

Bard told story after story to Stein, who was actually from Virginia instead of Germany. He was on the island for a wedding and to see the sights. Bard told him about the greatest sight there was, the most awesome act of creation in the world at the moment: the outpouring of red lava into the ocean at Kalapana.

"I can take you to a place where you stand on brand new rocks, still warm, like they're hot out of the oven. And if we go at night, all around you is this incredible huge pink fog that comes up when the lava pours into the water. You look up and the hills are full of these glowing golden lightning-cracks everywhere. And you look down and the red lava is pouring out into the ocean. It's creating new land right there, right at your fucking feet." He was into it; he was excited. "And you're right there, right there where it's all happening, just for you."

The goddess gasped. He had seen her work, had spoken with a reverence about it. He was not like the bands of others crawling over the rocks with their flashlights and their girlfriends and their coolers, to stand for a moment and say 'Oh, wow' and other foolish mortal things. He spoke of it as if he had seen the hand of God, which he had.

Stein agreed that it would be a good trip. He said he would like to go the following day. They continued to jostle downhill, as did the conversation, and Bard went off on his favorite subject, Tesla the magic mad scientist. It seems that Stein had a mild interest in electricity and that was more than enough to get Bard started.

"Nikolai Tesla was so far ahead of his time it's scary," he said. "He made a machine that produced lightning. Nobody took him seriously. They thought Edison had all the answers and they figured Tesla to be a crazy man, but he actually made lightning in his barn or something. You know, I'm working on this with Dwight in his garage, and I think we can reproduce the experiment if we just can come up with some of the materials—"

The goddess had never heard a man speak thus, had never imagined one who wanted to play with the elements. She followed all the way down the mountain, to Saddle Road again, to

Bard's house where they picked up some bottles of home-brewed beer, then to the last-Sunday-of-the-month cookout. When she saw the other people and heard the music from the radio, she slipped into the garden to listen a while longer. On her trip back home to the volcano, she had much on her mind.

The party, of course, was well underway by the time Bard and Stein showed up, dusty and starving from their trek. We threw the kabobs back on the grill to heat them up and shared some of their funny-tasting beers. Bard starting explaining how they were made, what exactly was in them, and how his friend was going to start a microbrewery in Hilo, but everybody was more interested in their trip up and down the mountain in the Neon.

He ate quietly for a while. I was glad to see him eat, because he looked even thinner than last time. He brought out the mother in me, and I thought it would be OK to have a son if he were like Bard. He and Dwight got along; they had a lot in common; they could be friends and work on things together. He would bring energy and ideas into the house, and we could feed him and commiserate when his love life didn't work out and rejoice with him when it did. We could encourage him to write about his adventures and follow through on any one of his inventions.

Since Stein was the newcomer, everybody was asking him questions. Bard looked a little distant.

"Ready for coffee?" I asked him.

"Yes" he said, and smiled.

"Cream and sugar and three ice cubes, right?"

"Yes." He was pleased that I remembered and that pleased me. He liked the ice cubes because he liked to drink the coffee

fast. When I put it in front of him he said thank you very politely, as if I had done him a great favor. He knew how to talk to
women, I thought at that moment. He had a great affection for
women and was growing up to be a good man. I would like to
be at his wedding. I would like to meet his children. It was a lot
to think about while placing a cup of coffee on a table.

"Did you want dessert?" I asked. "We don't have anything
nearly as good as the strawberry thing you made last time, but
there is chocolate cake, and Shelly made a pie."

"In the sky by and by?" he asked Shelly and she giggled. She
loved to bake and we first knew Bard as a baker. He was an assistant then, but a good one. "I'd love a piece of pie," he said and
she jumped up to serve him. She watched his reaction carefully
and he knew it. He tasted carefully, closing his eyes and taking
his time with every bite. "Mmm," he said. "How do you make
your crust so fine?"

Oh she was happy, and they talked about piecrusts and fresh
fruits and measuring cups and baking pans for a long time, drawing the other women into the conversation and branching out to
cakes and tortes and local things, *manapua*.

I remembered Bard the baker. He looked so funny in his tall
paper hat and clunky wooden shoes. He would burst through
the door of the cafeteria, both hands full of plates. He ate everything in a huge rush, talking about various disasters and suc-
cesses in the pastry shop.

"We made 600 rum balls this morning," he said once. "I bet
the Filipinos five bucks each that we couldn't finish by
lunchtime."

He got suspended one time for setting the kitchen on fire, trying to make lava out of sugar. It started when he accidentally let a
batch of caramel burn to a bubbling, oozing black mess, which
stayed hot and elastic for a long time. It so fascinated him that he

tried to recreate the experiment in a bigger pot. Unfortunately, Bard got distracted. It got away from him, started burning like hell and they couldn't put it out. They would've fired him except that he cleaned and repaired the burner on his own time and swore a solemn oath to never play mad scientist in the kitchen anymore. The pastry chef learned to keep Bard's time well occupied.

Most everybody left at some point after the re-telling of Bard's sugar lava experiment. He had gone off on another tangent, something about a new prescription drug that would increase the levels of dopamine in your system and thereby keep you young. He was working with a guy to procure it for a wealthy older lady he knew, who would thus be so grateful she would sponsor one of his best inventions.

"Can I get some of that?" I asked.

"Sure," he said, and smiled. "Can I get some more coffee?"

I carried dishes upstairs along with the last bottle of home-brew and put it in the refrigerator. I served up more coffee and drank some myself. Dwight and Stein were talking about electricity, in depth. The Bard, atypically, was simply sitting. He was in a chair at the corner of the table, just under the garage light. His chin was raised and he was pretending to listen but his eyes were glazed over like marbles. I wondered if he was thinking about his true love in California. He abruptly shook his head after a moment, as if talking himself out of something.

"There's always an alternative," I said. I don't know why I said that particular thing at that moment, but I'm sure that's what I said.

"Yes, there is," said Bard. "There's always an alternative. But that's the problem you see. In any situation where you have to make a decision there can be so many alternatives. The trick is to pick the right one at the right time."

"Well," I said, turning philosophical, "I have learned that

whatever you do, if you do it in a loving way it's harder to make a mistake." I had no idea what we were talking about but I knew this statement to be true.

"What would love do?" he said.

"What?" I asked.

"What would love do?" he said again. "That's how I put it. What would love do in the situation? If you put more love into it, what would that do to the situation?"

Stein was half listening to us. "Are we discussing the meaning of life here?" he asked.

"No," said Bard. "That's way too serious. Besides life doesn't have any meaning."

"Are you so sure?" asked Stein.

"Sure I'm sure," he answered. "We can't know the consequences of our actions. We just go along, enjoy life, dig out of it as much as we can and then die. If we stopped and thought about everything we were going to do, we'd never do anything. You have to go for it. That's it."

"Have you ever wanted to write a book?" I asked him.

"No," he said, "I don't want a following. I don't see myself as any kind of a guru or anything. I just like to take people on trips."

"But if you have something valuable to share, don't you think that you should?"

"What would love do?" he said.

I looked at him, so confident, yet fragile at the same time and realized that was why I cared about him so much. He was so much contradiction wrapped in one skinny body—the innocent derelict, the hysterical scientist, the philosopher who said "I dare you." I wondered for a moment if he would ever make up his mind which way to go. I didn't know how to answer the question for him. He didn't seem to mind.

The pull of the electricity conversation was too strong; the pause for philosophy was over. He was back into the debate about Tesla and Edison and A/C D/C and who knows what. I gave up and went to bed, leaving the three of them to argue over the answers for a long time more. Much later I heard them saying their goodnights, closing the garage door and driving away. Dwight came to bed and we agreed it was another successful party.

"The Bard seemed more pensive than usual," Dwight said. "Wonder what he's working on now."

"Whatever it is, I'm sure it will be amazing," I said. "With a brain like that."

"Yeah," said Dwight, "If only he would apply it to something—go ahead and study something and follow through on it. He's always got a new scheme. What do you suppose would happen if he ever really put his heart and soul into any one thing?"

What would love do? I thought.

The goddess couldn't sleep. She had never heard a man, especially such a young man, talk like that. He had wisdom and vision; he had passion, humor. She wanted him. She heard him say he was coming to the volcano the following night. She would see him, and at the very least he would alleviate her boredom and inspire her fantasy. Already she was dreaming, falling into rivers of sweet black lava, consuming it as fast as they could create it. Together they were burning everything in their way and racing crazily towards an ocean of electricity where they would make endless steam and the steam would make endless lightning, illuminating her island for all the world to see.

Bard woke up slowly the next morning. He stretched and let the dog out, showered and decided to forego shaving. He wrapped a towel around his waist, lit a Camel and walked out onto the front porch. He stretched and watched the dog run in the yard. *She is so beautiful,* he thought. She was a young Doberman, sleek and dark and full of life. He loved to watch her run. He had trained her to fetch coconuts, which he tossed like footballs for her. He fetched himself a cup of coffee and watched her playing in the early sunlight, enjoying her energy, her abandon. She rolled in the wet grass under the mango tree and shook her stub of a tail for him.

Bard looked up high into the tree remembering Ku'uipo, the blue and gold macaw that lived most of her daylight hours there until she disappeared. He raised her from an egg almost, and he had spent way too much time with her when she was young. They loved each other then as now, even in her absence. He never knew what happened, assumed some nice people drove by, held out an arm and she got on expecting a piece of papaya or a mac nut. Then the car sped away. He was teaching her to talk, to say *howzit* and aloha. She kept him company everywhere, and he could not look at the mango tree without thinking of her. He thought about cutting it down.

The dog came in the house and he explained why she could not go to the volcano this afternoon. It was too long a drive, two or three hours, and it would be hot and there was no water and she would be just too bored. He would come back late that night. He fed her and stroked her long, glorious nose.

He then packed up a knapsack with water, a flashlight, an extra pack of Camels, his pocket knife, a flannel shirt in case it got cold, sunglasses and sunblock. As long as the weather was good and the road was dry, he could drive through the first bunch of gates—to which he had the keys. After that, there was a trail that took them close to the flow. The forecast was good. He picked up a couple of mangos from the yard and put them in the knapsack.

He got on the phone, recruiting a few more volunteers for the trip into the park. It was going to be awesome, like nothing they had ever seen before. He would pick up Stein at the gas station in his uncle's Blazer and meet the others in Hilo about four. They'd be well inside the park by five. It was a short drive through a few gates and then about an hour's hike to the coast. From there they would have the best vantage point in the world of new lava as it poured into the ocean that night.

"Bring water," he advised, "and whatever else you like to drink, and a flashlight. And wear good shoes. No rubber slippers." The group grew to eight people before he left the house, just prior to which he called Helena's number in California. "It's Bard, just calling to say hi," he said to her machine.

The goddess started her day slowly as well. She stretched and watched wave after wave crash into the jagged black coast. She yawned and breathed in the sulfur steam of her handiwork. *Glorious,* she thought. She rolled over and looked at the new *pu'u,* the little hill, constructed during her night's dreams. From this mound a human eye could see everything, the very plunging and penetration of liquid rock into ocean. She was ecstatic. This was impressive. Thirty feet below the *pu'u* she had hung a shelf of rock. Its angle curved away from the wind, allowing one brave human to experience the very most intimate aspect of all. He could almost touch her essence from such a place, almost be a part of this, unseen and secret. Alone.

She went for a swim and from the far reaches of cooler waters observed the process. It was good work. He would have to be impressed. She exercised and ate some fish and floated back to the black sand shore.

Later, the goddess watched Bard and his little tour group make their way along the lava trail. She raised a breeze and blew a light overcast to cool the way, but even so it was not easy going. The new rock was brittle and broke under their steps, making shards that cut sneakers and tired feet. The trace of a trail was completely barren, black on black, rock on rock. It offered no diversion and no points of reference, but Bard knew the way. He kept them moving with promises that it would be well worthwhile, and they reached the edge of the *pali* just before sunset.

The lights of the volcano intensified, grew into a celestial glow of pink and gold as the sky darkened. Bard and his troupe lay on the warm rock and gazed into the steamy light until their eyes watered but could still make out a redder, brighter fire farther down. Some of the girls were moved to tears and one took off her clothes and sat on her shoes to get closer to the intensely cosmic energy. Stein leaned back, enjoying the view. He had another beer and declared it the most spiritual moment of this life.

Bard, standing, unsatisfied, said "Look, see the *pu'u* over there? If we climb up we can get upwind of the steam clouds, and watch the main flow going into the ocean. We can see everything from up there."

The group declared this position awesome enough. Coolers were re-opened and more beers passed around. Somebody brought out a guitar and they settled into the space. "I'm going up," said Bard after pacing for a while. "Come on." Then he took his flashlight and left.

The goddess was elated as she watched him separate himself from the boring group of immature mortals. *Yes*, she thought, *I have something to show you.* As he reached the top of the steep hill, she sighed and the steam clouds lifted a little higher, revealing what he had come to see.

It was as if the goddess had opened up her very heart and poured out the incandescent essence of her blood before his eyes. It was a perfect red arc from the cliff into the sea, and in the dark ocean he could follow the glow of it down and down to where it cooled and hardened into rock. The island stretched and grew in front of him. Life was forming at its most elemental level. It was creation, invention. He leaned forward.

His pale *haole* eyes glazed with tears from the smoke, but he couldn't look away from the hypnotic red glow. *It just goes down,* he thought, *forever.* The lava streamed down into the black void of ocean, disappearing and transforming, becoming what it must become. The goddess laughed with delight.

The guitar music stopped. The group was very quiet, listening to something they thought they heard. "What time is it?" someone asked. They realized Bard had been gone for a long time and called out to him. It was very black and very still. The steam clouds, in absence of wind, settled around them thickly, muffling sound further, disorienting them in a pink fog. Stein wanted to go look for Bard but they talked him out of it.

"Which direction?" somebody asked. "You could walk right off the cliff."

"He'll be back," said someone else.

They waited.

That was Monday. On Tuesday's evening news, there was a one-truck accident on Nimitz Highway, which tied up traffic in Honolulu; the Rainbow Wahine had defeated Tulsa again; and a hiker was missing in Volcanoes National Park. We didn't pay much attention. Hikers were always missing in the park.

Helicopters had explored seventeen miles of coastline up and down from the point of the flow. The Coast Guard was searching with boats. Agents on foot had combed the immediate area in daylight hours. Park police, fire & rescue, local cops and volunteers were on the scene. We figured it must be some camper with an ounce or two of *pakalōlō*, freaking out with the invasion of drug police.

That was at six o'clock. By the ten o'clock news, they had found a flashlight on the shelf of rock below a cinder cone. It had a name on it. It was Bard's.

Dwight got on the phone to a friend with connections in the police department. No, he had not heard. Yes, he would call back if he could verify anything.

"You know," I told Dwight. "He's probably drinking with

some campers in Puna. Probably walked himself out and got drunk and never bothered to call anybody to let them know."

"I don't know," said Dwight, "After two days . . ." The phone rang, and he got up to answer. " . . . although it would make a great story."

The friend with the police connections called back. Yes, it was Bard that was missing. No, they didn't have any answers. The park people and the police were none too happy with him in the first place for crossing private property and taking other people with him. They were likely to call off the search tomorrow.

My mind was racing. Who could we talk to to convince them to keep looking? Certainly he was still out there. I could see his thin body shivering in the wet wind, if it rained. Trapped in a crevice and unable to call out, if he had fallen. I pushed those images back. Not Bard.

The next day at work, I made some calls to friends of my boss, people with connections, with influence. I asked if they had heard about the lost hiker in the park, and did they know who I could call to give him one more day? I said he was only twenty-six years old and that he would find a way to stay alive until he was found. Those people were no help.

I called a friend who's an architect and lives in Volcanoes National Park with her husband, the historian. They know things. They know people. They know the goddess, and she is my last resort.

"The hiker in the park is a friend of mine," I began. I hardly had to finish the story.

"Let me make some calls and I'll get back to you." When she did, she did not have good news.

He had gone farther than he was supposed to go, climbed onto a cinder cone above the flow. He must have dropped on to a ledge thirty feet below that, and there were footprints in the new black sand, in a circle. There was the flashlight. He had fallen off or been washed into the ocean by a wave.

"You know," my friend said. "The ocean is very deep there." She chose her words carefully. "And it just goes down." She took a breath. "They brought Bard's father to the site," she said, and I was grateful that she used his name. "And he went with the rescue team. He insisted on rappelling down the cliff face himself. From what they saw, they believe there was no possibility." She spoke simply, factually. "And that he's gone."

When a goddess falls in love, the universe must align itself with her wishes. When she draws a man to her, when she calls his name and brings him to the very point of creation, the very point of life and death, what choice can he have? Is there always an alternative? What would love do?

Love would plunge into the boiling water. Love would see her eyes in the bottom of the sea and know that when she reached for him with the salty, rushing wave of her hand, he would go. He would live with her in and on and of the island he loved more than his own heart, and cook for her and tell her stories and make her laugh for the next thousand years.

In the back of the refrigerator in our house, there is a plain brown bottle of homebrewed beer. It was brought to us by the Bard of Hāmākua on the last Sunday of the month.

And there is a story inside.

THE FISHING CLUB

Kalani cupped his hand around the Zippo to block the sharp breath of wind—*ka makani*, his grandmother had taught him—that whipped down the hill on this part of the island. He had left the pickup in the driveway at home and parked his wife's old Dodge at Kishimoto Store so nobody would recognize him right away. He lit a cigarette for company while he waited for Hiro.

He surveyed the stars and mentally congratulated Hiro for picking a good night. The moon, three-quarters full, was lifting off the shoulders of the mountain and it would hang bright and blue overhead long enough to light their way down and back. The wind was good too. If anybody did happen to be close by, they wouldn't hear the group over the moans and groans of wind.

He took a long drag on the cigarette, exhaled downwind. The smoke vanished seaward. There were no boats, as usual, and that was good too. Kalani was glad for these things; they gave favorable signs for the job, and made him feel a little better. He had reservations, that was for sure, but the others had convinced him it was the right thing to do, and that it might work. He leaned back against the warm hood of the Dodge, tried to smoke peacefully and waited for the rest to get there. He knew he was early, as always. He watched for shooting stars.

After a little while the phone in the phone booth rang. Ronald was just leaving home, and he had the stuff. A little chicken skin crawled up Kalani's forearm, but it was too late to be nervous. Ronald would pick up Hiro and they would be there in ten minutes. Kalani hung up and took another look around. The old Kishimoto Store was on the main road to the resorts on the coast. It had sat here on its own as long as Kalani could remember, in the middle of acres of *kiawe* scrub brush. It had the one public phone that always worked and the little parking lot for watching the sunset and listening to the radio. He remembered stopping by the place when he was a much younger man, before cruising up the hill to town, sometimes with a girl, or meeting the boys for a few beers. Traffic passed up and down the road, like a diamond bracelet coming towards him and a ruby bracelet going away, stretched and ready to break apart.

Too many damn cars, he said to his cigarette. *It used to be dark here at night.*

He watched a flock of single headlights come his way. The motorcycle club growled toward him in staggered single file. *And quiet,* he thought. One of the headlights peeled off as Dwayne and Ellen Hicks pulled into the parking lot. *They're too old for ride the bike,* Kalani thought, but they were *haole* so they didn't care, and he didn't expect them to listen. They were fun to have around and even at sixty they liked to suck 'em up and talk story with the rest of the fishing club. Dwayne had adapted the bike a couple years ago after Ellen's hip surgery, when she couldn't straddle the big Harley anymore. So now she had an ingenious sidecar, lovingly crafted out of a canoe.

"Hey, *howzit*, Kalani? I thought you quit smoking." Ellen rushed up to him for a kiss on the cheek and he obediently crushed the Camel out on the gravel.

"My grandchildren, they give me hell," he said, shuffling his feet, "But I tell them if they live long enough to do something for fifty-seven years they deserve to keep doing it too."

"You still make love to your wife, don't you?" laughed Dwayne as he settled the bike. He waved at the passing fleet of motorcycles and signed off on his radio, replacing it in the caddy.

"Well I still make love, but never mind with who." Kalani chuckled and affectionately rubbed the fender of the old brown Dodge. "Hey, what did you bring that motorcycle for? Anybody's gonna know it's you folks."

"Kalani, you worry too much. I told you, anybody asks, we tell them we went fishing, just like always," said Ellen.

"Yeah, but we never met here and parked here before."

"Yeah, well this time we did," said Dwayne, ending the argument. He pulled his knapsack off the bike and produced a folding shovel, flashlights, a canteen. "Here, take a little shot of courage. Where's everybody?"

Kalani took a pull on the canteen and passed it to Ellen. "Jimmy's wife is sick and she won't let him out. Ronald and Hiro are on the way. Stanley got called into work."

Dwayne spat on the ground. "When's that man going to retire? What's he been there, thirty years? Does he think the place will blow up if he leaves? They'll have to drag him out of that hotel kicking and screaming or else bury him right there in the boiler room floor."

"Well you know him, yeah?" said Kalani, refusing a second turn at the canteen. "He talks to the machines. Started doing it right after you and I left. He has names for the boilers, and my son says he talks to them just like they was people."

"He always was crazy," Dwayne said. "Remember that time the boiler room flooded and he wouldn't let Housekeeping in until he took down all the nudie pictures?" They laughed. Kalani felt better. He usually did around these two. They had a way of doing that.

More headlights came into the lot, but it was a young man they didn't know, stopping to use the phone. They recognized the bellman's uniform from one of the hotels and nodded hello.

"So where's your fishing things?" Kalani asked loudly.

"Here, here," said Ellen. She pulled rods and nets out of the canoe, and a small cooler. Kalani made Dwayne stow the shovel back in his knapsack and lit another cigarette.

"So as soon as the rest gets here we can go fishing!" Kalani said.

"Yeah," said Dwayne, "Where's your stuff?"

Kalani, very businesslike, walked to the back of the car and looked blankly at the spot where, had this been his truck, the tackle box would be. The bellman finished his call and drove away. Kalani still stared at the trunk of his wife's car; Dwayne and Ellen cracked up laughing. Finally, Ronald's truck pulled in with no headlights on. He and Hiro and Hiro's grandson James piled out calling hello to everyone like always.

"Shh, shh!" Kalani said, "No names, remember? Don't say anybody's names!"

Ronald patted him on the head. "There's nobody around, Kalani. Who's gonna hear us, Kalani?" (Kalani muttered under his breath.) "What did you say, Kalani?"

"I said no names, and no kids. What did you bring him for? This is dangerous what we're doing!"

"That's why I brought him," said Hiro. "If there's watchdogs over there, James can run for help while they're eating you, and the rest of us might have a chance." Everybody laughed except Kalani.

"Watchdogs?" he asked, nervous again. "Ellen, do you have any meat at your house? Run home and—"

"There's no dogs," said Ronald. "Hiro been over there plenty, days and nights, and there's nothing except one gate."

"Yes," said Hiro. "James and I been fishing there almost everyday—just like we said—and there's nothing over there. No fish either. His mom thinks we're crazy but I keep telling her you caught the biggest *menpachi* of your life over there, and I'm gonna beat you!"

"Me?" Kalani was tired of being teased and the moon was up and ready; so was he.

"Where's your fishing things, Kalani?" asked Ronald. He threw his knapsack and poles into the back of his truck.

"Shut up," said Kalani. "Here's *ti* leaf." He took a KTA bag from the back seat and passed it around, instructing them each to take one and keep it with them tonight. James asked why and he told him it was for good luck.

Ronald unfolded a greasy piece of paper from his pocket. "OK," he said, "let's look at the list."

If there were bears in Hawai'i or Portugal, these were Ronald's ancestors. His size gave him instant authority in their group, and had for twenty years. Divorced years ago, he lived alone near the beach and still worked at the hotel where they all had at one time or another. He kept an eye on crazy Stanley and his boilers and he brought all the fresh gossip to his retired friends in the fishing club.

"Shovel, flashlight, fishing things. Bolt cutters?" Kalani had them. "You got your locksmith tools, Dwayne?"

"Yep."

Dwayne would cut the padlock off the chain link fence and switch cylinders with a brand new Master padlock while the rest were digging. He would put the old cylinder in the new padlock and re-lock the gate when they left. The construction crew would come in the morning and open the gate just like always. Nobody would know anyone had been inside.

"Beer?"

Ellen patted the cooler. "And more back at our house when we're *pau*."

"OK, anything else?"

"Where's the stuff?" asked Kalani.

"In the truck," Ronald said. He re-folded the list, put it back in his pocket.

"I want to see it," Kalani said; everyone paused and looked at Ronald. This had more or less been his idea from the beginning, and no one had really wanted to know where "the stuff" was going to come from. Ronald said he knew, and that was good enough for them. The fun had been the planning—sitting around the park drinking icy beers and watching the turtles pop their heads out of the water like little submarines. They had spent many evenings pleasantly arguing over the plan, the place, the time. "The stuff" had just been something that Ronald was bringing, like the bolt cutters and the beer.

Now here it was, real. Ronald looked at their faces, especially James', whose eleven-year-old eyes were wide as the moon. James had seen grownups, even his idolized Grampa, act nervous and spooky before, but usually they were pretending—trying to scare him. This time they were not.

"You sure?" Ronald paused ominously. They nodded.

Kalani spoke up bravely. "Yeah, for all we know you dug up your old dog and brought his bones."

"Dog bones don't look like human bones," said Ellen. "That wouldn't work."

"Well maybe he dug up his ol' ex-mother-in-law."

Ronald snickered. He had loved the dog. "OK," he said. "Come here."

They walked over to the truck and stood around it looking into the bed. Among the usual clutter of gear was an old burlap bag. "Get the flashlight, James." Ronald's massive fingers untied the knot and pushed the sides of the bag down. On cue, the wind howled and the moon hid behind a small cloud. James' hand made the flashlight beam tremble as it scanned the pile of long, curved and knobby objects that could easily have been rocks or coral, except for the human skull in the center of the pile.

"What's that?" asked James.

Ronald picked it up and turned its grinning face to James. "You mean *who's* that." There was a bullet-size hole through the middle of its forehead. Ronald tossed it to James, who yelped and ducked, then hid under the truck. Dwayne caught the skull.

Kalani hung onto the truck with one hand and crossed himself with the other, saying a fast prayer to Jesus, Mary and Joseph and any of the saints who might be available. The rest were transfixed, except Dwayne, who held up the skull and recited Shakespeare. "Alas poor Horatio. I knew him well . . ." until Ronald smacked him on the shoulder and Ellen said, "Yorick."

Again, headlights turned into the parking lot, and this time it was a police car. Ronald covered the bones back up, and sensing his band was near panic said, "Everybody get in the back of the truck, nice and calm. James, come on out now and help them. Kalani, you get up front."

The policeman pulled right up behind them and got out of the car with his big flashlight panning the area. "You folks need any help?" Everybody froze. Kalani nearly fainted. He gave up on the saints and called on the family *'aumakua*, asking for just strength enough to lift his leg up into the cab.

"Oh hi, Uncle." The cop put down the light and walked over to shake hands with Ronald.

"Walter!" said Ronald. "How's that car running since we rebuilt the carburetor?"

"Some fast, Uncle Ronald. Thanks again."

"What time you get off, Walter? You like go fishing with us?" The truck began to quiver on its tires.

"Oh, I'm off now. I just stopped here to take the light off." Those in the truck, who had started breathing again when they heard the word "Uncle," now gripped the sides of the truck and looked heavenward, as if they could somehow levitate it and blow away with the wind. Walter and Ronald went over to the Trooper, unbolted the police light from the top, then stowed it in the back. It was a blessing that Kalani, who had finally managed to get himself into the front seat, couldn't hear the conversation. James stared at the burlap bag. Finally Ronald and Walter shook hands again and Walter drove away.

"Don't worry so much! Walter's family hates to go fishing," Ronald said. "Ready to go?" He hoisted up behind the wheel and started the truck down the road.

It was a way to the entrance of the construction site, a bumpy windy ride for the folks in back. They pulled off onto the shoulder and waited 'til there was no traffic in either direction. Then Ronald maneuvered the big Ford to one side, off the road and around the chain which loosely guarded the entrance. He drove slowly down the gravel road to the place where the new hotel was being built. Ronald turned off the headlights when the moon came back out and in a couple of minutes, they could see the flashing safety lights of the cranes like red-eyed dinosaurs reaching their long necks out of the pit.

When they were close enough, Ronald turned the truck around, facing *mauka* for a quick getaway, and stopped the engine. The dust was swept away by the wind.

Kalani spoke for the first time since the cop had come. "This is crazy," he said. "We have to go back."

"No," said Ronald, as he climbed down out of the truck.

"We're gonna get caught," Kalani said. "We're gonna get

caught for trespassing and go to jail!" He began the process of lowering his feet, then legs, then torso to the road. *When had Ronald lifted his truck up so high?* he thought.

"Shut up," said Ronald, slamming the tailgate open.

"James, help them with their things," said Hiro, again unperturbed. "Kalani, we all agreed that it was time to do something besides talk, so here we are. Have you changed your mind? Do you want them to build this hotel?"

Kalani searched for his Zippo. "No, but I don't want to go to jail either. Besides, this isn't going to really stop them. It's their land now; they paid for it and they don't care about bones. They'll just move them if they do find them, or plow right over like the other hotels did."

"That's true," said Hiro. He produced a match to light his friend's cigarette. "It probably won't do any good."

"Yeah, Kalani," said Dwayne as he helped Ellen climb down off the tailgate. "They probably won't even find them, like you said. It won't make any difference."

"There's already too many goddam hotels anyway," said Ronald. "Too many goddam golf courses, too many cars, too many people."

"That's right." Kalani nodded vigorously. "It's already too late!" Hiro nodded too, and handed him the bolt cutters.

"That's right," said Ronald. "Three years ago they didn't have enough people for the jobs in the hotels, and now they're building more of them at the same time they're laying us off."

Dwayne shouldered the knapsack and Ellen carried the cooler. Everyone was almost agreeing with each other that this was a futile waste of time as they moved toward the pit.

At the chain link fence Dwayne took the bolt cutters ceremoniously from Kalani, and snapped off the padlock. Holding the cut lock in the tool's jaws, he kicked the big gate open for his wife and his friends. He gave them a militant nod, slipped out of the knapsack and unrolled the pouch of locksmithing tools. "I'll be down in a minute," he said to Ellen. She gave him a little good luck pat on the back and picked up the knapsack.

They sneaked around the pit to the north wall, the place Hiro and James had reconnoitered on their way to the fishing spot. The construction work exposed a lava tube, causing the dig to stop, so they could collapse then re-pack the tube. Hiro knew this could have been a natural mausoleum for Hawaiians anyway, and he knew this was the perfect place and time to do their planting.

Hiro was thinking about planting while they made their way. He had been a groundskeeper at the hotel for twenty-one years, working alongside other members of the fishing club. They had always been proud of their jobs, proud of the place where they worked.

How many bushes had he planted in that time? How many strawberry guavas or sweet tangerines had he given to the guests' children or their children's children? How much of himself was left there growing in those gardens, and would the boys that came after him remember how much to water, how much to fertilize, how much to prune? His life work was growing things, and now he would try to stop a whole hotel from growing. He thought to himself and shook his head, *Weeds*.

They gathered at the designated corner and Hiro looked down in. They were too late.

"Oh no," he said. "They must have blasted out the whole tube. Or else it was a lot smaller than it looked. Let me have the flashlight, James." The beam showed a straight vertical wall dropping into blackness. Hiro looked woeful.

"I told you," said Kalani.

"Shut up," said Ronald.

"It's OK, Grampa," said James.

"There must be another spot we can bury them," said Ellen, always pragmatic.

"Where?" demanded Kalani. "This is as far as they're gonna dig! Where can we put them now so somebody will find them?"

"Shut up and let me think," said Ronald, and they did. Dwayne came up, his job finished and the lock ready to replace.

"What's the problem?" He evaluated the situation, half-listening to their explanation, and looked around the site slowly. "Are you sure they're not gonna dig anymore?" he asked Kalani.

"Yes. Absolutely. My cousin drives the cement truck and they're coming in for the first big pour next week," he answered.

"Ronald," said Dwayne, "Didn't you tell me they're gonna tear down all these rock walls?"

"That's what I hear," said Ronald. "Couple years ago, before any of this, that professor from UH and a bunch of archaeologists from the mainland came out here and did a survey. They decided that all these walls," he waved both hands in the wind, "were just something farmers put up for their gardens, and they weren't important to save. So Mr. Johnson, the contractor, is gonna tear them all down. They're not very good Hawaiian walls anyway. You can tell because the rocks don't fit together right, see? My grandfather worked on the walls down in—"

"OK!" said Dwayne. "Let's put the stuff under one of these walls, and when they knock the wall down, they'll find Mr. Bones."

Kalani shook his head. "Hawaiian people would never build a wall on top of a grave, and they would never dig a grave under a wall."

Dwayne was undeterred. "No, they wouldn't, but this guy has a bullet through his head, and besides we don't know if he's Hawaiian or what."

"He's Hawaiian," said Ronald.

"OK, OK," said Dwayne, "So somebody shot him, and hid him under this wall. OK? How old are the bones?"

"Old," said Ronald.

"And how old are the walls?" Ronald shrugged.

"OK, we're here. We got everything together. Let's just do it. What have we got to lose? What do you think Hiro?"

"I think," he said, calm again, "That we ought to go over to that wall and drink a beer." That was an acceptable suggestion, the best part of which was that they could go outside the fence, put Dwayne's padlock in place and breathe easier. Sitting on a wall, beers or no beers, bones or no bones, was a lot less scary than trespassing on the foundation of the new hotel. James was particularly relieved, and—the first one out the gate—he found a suitable *kiawe* tree to pee behind. The wind had calmed too, and the bright moon seemed to agree with their decision. Dwayne clicked the lock neatly in place, then as an afterthought wiped it and the chain with the edge of his T-shirt.

They selected one of the closer, more dilapidated stone structures, V-shaped. There were six beers in the little cooler so Ellen gave one to James too, and Hiro didn't say anything. They drank together under the stars as they had done for so many years.

"So, Ronald," she finally asked, "Tell us where you found the bones."

Ronald sat on the flattest available stone and sipped on his beer. "I won't tell you where," he said, "But they're real, and they're Hawaiian. My grandfather used to tell me about this secret graveyard up in the hills where our family was buried. And one night, when I was about James' age, he took me up there to the caves. It was dark, not like this, and no wind. Everything was still, and cool and very quiet—no birds, no lizards chirping, no cars. We had to hike off the road in this pasture, and the grass was wet, and to me it was deep. It rubbed on my legs like fingers or something." He rubbed James' leg with one big hand, damp from the cold beer can.

"And in the middle of the field was a rise and a crack in the ground where there was one lava tube. It was dark as hell, and Grampa said to go inside there, but I wouldn't go first, so he crawled in with the flashlight and I held onto his belt with my eyes closed and never let go. We crawled for a long ways and then he turned the light out and started to chant in Hawaiian, but I didn't understand what he was saying so I got really scared and started to cry. He told me to open my eyes, but I couldn't because I was too scared, so he got all piss off with me and said 'Go' so I backed out of there as fast as I could and just sat there in the grass outside for a long time until he came out. And you know what he had in his hand? This guy right here."

Ronald reached into the sack and pulled out the skull. His audience gasped. "He said, 'This is your great-great-great-grand-father, and he's shame that you're such a coward. But he says one day you're gonna need him, and when you do, he'll be waiting for you right here.' And he took the head and he rolled it back into the lava tube and there was—Poof!—this big flash of light, like lightning inside there. And he would never take me back again, no matter how much I begged."

Ronald handed the skull to James who held it, awed, in both hands, peering into the bullet hole. "Who shot him? he asked.

"Who knows?" was Ronald's reply. He finished his beer and crushed the can. "Let's get to work."

They moved a small section of the wall at its V and tried to dig out underneath, but the camp shovel, intended to work in the soft dirt at the site, was practically useless in the thin hard soil. They managed to make a depression big enough for the skull and had to settle for covering up the remaining bones with rocks and some sandy dirt they scraped up. It looked realistic enough in the dark and it was getting very late.

As they turned to go back to Ronald's truck, somebody suggested that a prayer would be a good idea. Ronald didn't feel like it so they asked Kalani to pray since he had the most Hawaiian blood anyway.

"Heavenly Father," he began, "We brought these old bones down here from their rightful place up *mauka*, and we didn't mean any disrespect by it. We ask your forgiveness and we ask their forgiveness, and we hope that we didn't do anything too bad to upset the other spirits here by the ocean, and the ones up there in the cave. We are sorry for interfering, but we did it for try and stop them from building this hotel, because we think our island has enough, and people have to speak up about that because we're the ones here on earth right now. We don't think that Ronald's great-great-great-grandfather would have minded helping us. Thank you. Mahalo. Aloha. Amen."

They loaded the truck and went back to their vehicles. The moon was low on the horizon over the ocean. Nobody really felt like drinking anymore, so they shook hands and Ellen kissed cheeks all around. Kalani took out one smoke for the drive home, then remembered his wife didn't allow smoking in her car. He put the cigarette back in the pack and back in his shirt pocket and noticed the lighter wasn't there, but didn't think anything of it. He was tired. They all went home and so did the moon.

Nothing happened for three days. Then Kalani heard from his cousin that the big concrete pour had been postponed, and the fishing club called a meeting to exchange information. Nobody had much and the general consensus was to wait some more. Nobody had Kalani's lighter either, which bothered him, and he had already been by the Kishimoto Store to look for it. Hiro and James went fishing by the site as usual. They took turns spying and fishing one whole afternoon from after school 'til dark. Unfortunately that day they were really biting and the two spies returned home with a five-gallon bucketful of fish and not much information.

By the end of the week, the pour was scheduled again. Kalani's cousin revealed that the delay was only due to some equipment being delivered from the mainland. Ronald went down and applied for a job with one of the contractors. He managed to nose around and find out that while they were waiting for the concrete, Mr. Johnson was anxious for the crews to be occupied. He directed his foremen to clear the entire area of rock walls, starting with those closest to the road and working their way *makai*. One by one they bulldozed the walls and put the rocks aside to make new walls around some of the landscaping.

A few more days passed, and then Stanley from the boiler room heard from the fuel oil man that all work had stopped, that the men assigned to the walls had walked off the site, refusing to come back to work. They found something. Bones.

It didn't take long for the news to get around the island, and with the news, hundreds of arguments over the ancestry and authenticity of the bones. A team of archaeologists, hired by the developer at great expense, descended on the area. They cordoned off the whole site with yellow tape and attacked the ground with whiskbrooms and teaspoons.

Native Hawaiian groups came with *ti* leaf-wrapped offerings and *lei* and chants and ceremonies. Several different groups of demonstrators claimed some relationship to the remains, or the ancestral burial ground. They camped nearby and made picket lines up and down the highway.

Of course reporters and TV crews made a camp of their own, while swarms of curious tourists and locals parked cars on the shoulder to get a look. They climbed the lava to peer over the yellow tape and hoisted children on their backs for a glimpse of something that might turn out to be historic or important, or worth talking about.

The developers insisted despite claims of the protesters, that a full archaeological survey had been completed prior to any construction. No historical or cultural sites of any significance were found. Mr. Johnson persuaded the police to rather quietly begin an investigation of their own. He wasn't sure what he suspected, but he was suspicious.

Questions were asked, through some of the same channels that the fishing club had used—the cement truck driver, the fuel oil man, Mr. Kishimoto at the store, fishermen, cousins, aunties, co-workers. All had opinions; all had theories, but the appearance of the bones was conspicuously mysterious.

An old *Kahuna* came down one morning to see for himself. He passed through the layers of observers undisturbed, and approached the V-wall deliberately, slowly, almost unnoticed, until he cast his bent and aged shadow onto the back of one archaeologist crawling along the wall's base with a paintbrush. The shadow froze him, instinctively made him cover his head and lay in the dust unmoving. The *Kahuna* was not looking at the worker or the wall. He stood like a *kiawe* tree, and watched the ocean as if waiting for a ship, silently.

In a moment he laid a wrinkled hand on the wall, feeling, then stopped and picked up a handful of earth and let it sift through his fingers. He shook his head. The prostrate archaeologist righted himself and showed the *Kahuna* the table where the bones had been placed for cataloguing, photographs and study. The *Kahuna* held up the skull and looked through its empty eyes at the blue sky. He smiled, replaced it, and walked away.

Kishimoto Store was booming. He could hardly stock enough sodas to keep up with the demand and his wife had started a brisk plate lunch business in the back. He had even rented half a dozen port-a-luas and got around the pay toilet law by selling Charmin by the yard. There was no place to park. The phone had been used so much that vandals finally thought it was worth their time to break in and steal the coin box. So for the first time anybody could remember, the pay phone at Kishimoto's was out of order.

The Kishimoto parking lot was crowded and all the beach parks were full of *malihini* campers from someplace else. The fishing club meeting was moved to the Hicks' house. They drank cold beers and cooked meat on the grill. Ellen put out a pot of rice and they listened to Kalani complain.

"It's more worse now!" he whined. "More people, more cars; you can't go fishing down there anymore; picket lines on the road; somebody broke the phone. We didn't fix anything. We made it worse."

"Kalani you sound like an old lady," said Ellen. She flipped the top and passed him another beer. "This will all settle down soon and people can get on with their lives."

"I don't think so," said Ronald. He emphasized the 'so' by swatting a mosquito on his arm. "My sister-in-law works for the construction company and she says if the developer has to pay for much more delays, they're gonna fold up and go back to the mainland, and if that happens, her company might go out of business."

"A lot of folks are gonna lose their jobs," Hiro added.

"That's right," said Kalani, "we messed with something we

should have left alone. We messed up, that's what we did!"

"So what you like do, Kalani?" Ronald said, "Take 'em back?"

For a minute the fishing club looked at each other in silence. Without saying it, they all wondered if this was a solution that would work. In the pause, a spatter of rain made polka dots on the picnic table, then stopped.

Hiro looked at the sky. "I'm going home," he said. "Don't ask me what I think anymore. You folks do whatever. I'm not saying it was a mistake, but—I'm going to stay home for a while."

Dwayne turned from the grill and plopped another plate of steak on the table. "No way," he said, as he waved goodbye to Hiro. "The deed is done. It was easy to go in before. It's damn near impossible to even go over there now."

"We made somebody angry and we have to make it right," Kalani said. He wiped a stray raindrop off the back of his neck.

"If you really want to make it right," said Ellen, "Let's go forward and tell the truth."

"What truth?" Ronald said. "That we broke into somebody's property and planted some bones in the ground? But really they lease it from the State, and the state stole it from the family that lived there before, that the king gave it to, and that king stole it from the chiefs before him. So whose land did we go trespass on? And what truth did you want to tell? That land doesn't belong to anybody except whoever happens to be there at the moment and right now that land belongs to those bones. So I say we let them stay right there and have their fun."

It began to rain in earnest and they scrambled inside with plates and pots and steaks and beers, leaving the grill to steam and sizzle alone.

Ronald drove home in the rain, grumbling to the windshield wipers. He had not told his friends about the conversation with his nephew, the cop. Walter called up and asked him about the night he ran into the fishing club at Kishimoto Store. He asked about the skull with the bullet hole, which he remembered from other campfires and other stories as a boy. Walter also let him know that the experts were almost *pau*. They had not found anything except the one series of bones, which they determined not only to be younger than the wall, but definitely brought there from someplace else. Dirt stuck in the crevices did not match the dry dust near the site. Police were now thinking more in terms of foul play than history, and there was talk of the FBI coming in. The archaeologists were giving up and turning the whole site over to the legal authorities. The picture was becoming very crowded, and he had almost decided, no he had decided, to let Walter take him in to the station.

It rained for two days and nights, one of those once-in-twenty-years Kona storms that beat down on the islands like an insane car wash. The archaeologists and demonstrators, the tourists and news people took a couple days off and calmness returned. All plans, including Ronald's, were on hold.

Early in the morning of the third day, Kalani drove down to Kishimoto Store for coffee and gossip. The island looked freshly painted, still damp in the new light of pre-dawn. He took note of small damage along the way: a tree down by the church, the flooded-out garage of a house on the *makai* side. The road was blocked by debris near Kishimoto Store, and most of the construction boys had been called in to help clear it.

Dwayne was there too. He sipped coffee from a styrofoam cup as he watched the bulldozers slowly push the rocks. He listened to the operators talk to each other on the CB. They shook hands and watched a while together. Kalani smoked a cigarette. They leaned on the motorcycle, and remembered driving the big machines; they remembered other times, other storms. They were interrupted by a squawk from the bike's radio. It broke through the usual radio patter as if some hand had snatched the mike from another.

"This is Johnson up at the site. I want everybody back here right now—and get the water truck with at least a hundred feet of water hose. Keep the heavy equipment on the road—do not go off the gravel until you talk to me. Got it? The Old Man is gonna be over here on the next flight, and he is not gonna believe this. Let's get moving, people."

"Let's go," Kalani said. "Your bike can get through."

"You sure?" Dwayne's eyes twinkled. Kalani had never before remotely considered the motorcycle as real transportation. Kalani stamped out the cigarette and Dwayne kicked the engine awake. Kalani allowed his curiosity to overcome his fear of the bike, and climbed into its outrigger. They passed easily by the road workers and down to the construction area, no traffic. Not much was left of the V-shaped wall where they sat and drank a beer that night. It felt like a long, long time ago.

A few people were there on the ground, crawling in the mud like a demolition derby for babies. Shouts of "Look over here!" and whoops and swearing in amazement cut through the air and the distant rumbling of the earthmovers. Dwayne drove right through the yellow tape and nobody looked up.

Amid the stooped crowd, a single upright figure stood by the wall, watching the sparkling ocean. It was the old *Kahuna*. He seemed very happy to see them and smiling, gestured them over. "Come," he called. "Look." As they walked towards him, one of Kalani's rubber slippers came off in the mud. When he peeled it up, the figure of a warrior, his spear raised, winked up at him from the rock beneath, then disappeared back into the oozing mud. Kalani knelt and wiped his hand over the lava rock, and a second warrior stood beside the first. *Petroglyphs! That's what they were looking at.*

The ground was literally crawling with crawling people, frantically wiping the rock, uncovering a whole panorama of carvings. There were acres of warriors, families, animals and plants, and new strange symbols and shapes they had never seen before—hundreds. In some places the bare rock revealed much more, and hints of structures, clues to foundations. The more expert an archaeologist was, the more excited and the more muddy he got as the pages of this ancient book began to turn.

Soon a parade of construction vehicles rolled back into the site with a fanfare of rumbles. Mr. Johnson looked around in amazement as the archaeologist in charge of the moment animatedly explained.

"The walls, remember? They were for agriculture. The farmers on this side of the island terraced the land to keep the soil from washing away during the worst storms, and when we moved the walls, and it rained—Look! Just look!"

The rainstorm had scoured more than two feet of topsoil off the lava in some places, revealing messages from a settlement much older than the gardens planted above it, much older than anything found on this island. It was inarguably the widest expanse of petroglyphs any of the university people had ever seen, and the symbols were so unusual, so many new ones to study, completely different from anything previously found anywhere in the island chain. This was a legend uncovered, an unimagined chapter of history predating history, buried long ago and forgotten by other Hawaiians in other times.

By the end of the day, the circus had come back to town, bigger and better than ever. The developer himself, Mr. Johnson's boss, came in person to the site and even he took off his shoes to walk out and touch the carvings in the rock. As he passed by he looked down into the foundation of his hotel and saw a tiny reflection of himself in the water at the bottom. Maybe he thought about how fleeting the reflection in the water was, compared to the one in stone.

The TV cameras showed him speaking about working together with the community towards whatever end was most beneficial to the citizens of yesterday, today and tomorrow. The news analysts said that meant he had great plans for a museum, a cultural park and a study center. They showed the whole site on TV, with all the muddy people and the mysterious civilization under their feet like ancient newspapers. The fishing club, watching TV together, cheered.

The cameras did not record a moment later, when the developer took a cigar out of his pocket and walked over to a remnant of rock wall to put his shoes back on. On the rock sat an old bent man, poking into the ground with an *o'o* stick. The developer was feeling very historical, very proud and male, as if he himself alone was responsible for this incredible discovery. When he sat on the wall, the old man asked, "And what have you found here today?"

The developer pointed with his cigar and crowed, "This is the most significant archaeological find on this island, ever." He waved one hand in the sun, and searched his pockets with the other. "I found the opportunity of a lifetime; a place in Hawaiian history!" He watched the old *Kahuna* scratch the *o'o* on the ground. "And what have you found here?" he asked.

"Zippo," the old *Kahuna* said. He snapped it open, and gave the man a light.

HALE HEAHEA

There was always a breeze through Hale Heahea, the welcoming home. Mornings it rolled down the mountains carrying with it smells of high country rains on fresh flowers. It swept aside any intruding clouds that threatened a perfect crescent beach, and cooled sunbathers and their *mai tai*. It refreshed arriving guests as they bowed to receive a *lei* at the *porte cochere*, then perfumed their rooms and lifted their spirits with the sweetest air of Hawai'i. Evenings, it rushed back with the mysterious scent of the sea, between the tall pillars of the lobby atrium, like the hotel staff *pau hana*—headed home from work.

Just before morning this day, the breeze slipped between the louvers into the General Manager's office. It ruffled reports on her desk and turned the heart-shaped faces of cream and green anthuriums in their crystal vase. She put down the heavy silver pen, rubbed her eyes and looked out. The moon was lowering into the ocean, unperturbed by the coming day.

She considered the disarray of papers before her; she knew what they said, but it didn't make any difference today. Hotel occupancy for the month prior to closing had not met projections. Energy was way up; exceptionally hot weather set three new peak demands for electricity. Penalties on payables, overtime, and allowances ate into the profit line like termites. The Profit & Loss Statement was not good news. They would have to wire funds from Tokyo to make the final payroll.

She leaned back in her chair, a joke from her father, which she had never given up. It was hand-carved *koa*, covered in leather the golden color of a local boy's skin. Its rich upholstery rolled across the back and arms forming not-too-subtle lines of a male torso. It had been her father's way of letting her know it was OK to be "so damned independent."

While she watched the ocean gradually lighten, she laid her cheek on the strong left shoulder and wondered when it would come, the grief. "At least this way you'll always have a shoulder to cry on," he had said. She reached across her chest to the bicep and clung for a moment, as she had done so often, to the chair, to him. There were no tears this morning, with too much to do and no time left. *How did this happen?* she thought.

The doors had opened on the day she was born. Created in a time when the rich were still respected and wealth was still aspired to, Hale Heahea stood as a flag, a symbol of The Best, when that still had definition. One of the great families had built it as if from dreamed blueprints, sparing no expense and over-looking no detail. To one of the most poetically beautiful beach-es in the world, in a climate as perfect as the earth can produce, they added a visionary landscape that would grow into a mas-terpiece. They built a revolutionary desalinization plant to take water from the sea by the millions of gallons, constructed a new road to the airport.

Magnificent, state-of-the-art kitchens came under the watchful

eyes of European chefs who, patiently for the most part, trained
the local people in the elegant art of preparing and serving food.
The golf course settled on the rolling grounds like a quilt made
from Ireland, and the building itself was no detraction from the
natural splendor. Rather it hung like Zen picture frames, accentu-
ating, drawing the viewer's eye to, emphasizing and teaching, the
priceless pictures of ocean, sky and growing things.

Superlatives in a dozen languages had been heaped upon the
place, yet its seduction remained indescribable. Writers called it
a work of art, and that's exactly what it was. Art imitating life,
quality life. It was an enormous stage set, completely fabricated
by its designers for the pleasure and comfort of honored guests.
When they started to arrive, the place became alive.

It was the the right place to be, at the right time.

It occurred to Roxanne that she had not yet packed her own
things to move out of Hale Heahea tonight, or made any
arrangements for where to go. There wasn't much, only clothes
and some books, personal things, the chair. The last six months
were too busy; time and energy could not be spared on surroundings. She had the guest bedroom next to the office fitted
with a connecting door, so work or rest were only steps from
each other, and moved in-house until it was over.

She slipped into her bedroom to begin preparations for this
day, and was surprised to see the fresh *ti* leaf *pu'olo* on her vanity *Where did that come from?* she thought. There was no card.
Somebody sent me a lei. I'll open it later.

She glanced in the closet to be sure housekeeping had
brought up the laundry, checked the floor for the right shoes,

opened a drawer and noted a new pair of nylons. Everything was in place. She undressed, started the shower water, then curiosity called her back to the vanity.

She opened the *pu'olo*. It *was* a lei—magnificent, unlike any she had seen before. Jade flowers and crown flowers wound together like a garland of precious gems, heavy, strong. She lifted and dropped it over her naked shoulders and looked in the mirror. For a moment she felt weak, as if she couldn't bear the weight. The moment passed.

She would save it for sunset, when Kahu blessed the property and they tied the *maile* across the front door. It would be good to have something beautiful and strong at that moment, and perhaps by then she would know its giver. Lighter, she took a fast shower, dressed and turned to the task of makeup. She hated the ritual of powders, brushes and pencils, but she practiced it faithfully. The mask was important; it would help her look composed today, presenting the cosmetic face they expected without revealing the lies and lines underneath. In the old days she would never have bothered. Before she took the road that brought her here.

From a very early age she had wanted to know how things worked. Huge things, things that made the world go round. Then she wanted to make them work better. As soon as she learned what the word meant, she told her somewhat baffled family, "I want to be an engineer when I grow up." It was her first and only goal.

"It's up to you," they said.

While her friends were practicing *hula* or learning to surf, she took apart watches and bicycles. After school, she ran down the street to Uncle's house and handed him wrenches while he worked on the neighborhood cars. Sometimes if he dropped a bolt, he'd let her squeeze her small hand in between the engine parts to snag it for him. She never failed to retrieve it, grinning and greasy to her chin. And he never failed to clean her up before he sent her home for dinner.

When her parents built their new house on the ocean, she was the one who talked the architect into turning the building on its lot to let the breeze blow through and keep the afternoon sun off the front windows. She watched the workmen every day, asking question after question, begging to help the plumbers or the carpenters or the concrete crew with their huge truck.

Her father came to the site one day and saw her on a ladder, high up against the rock wall under construction. A tan young man held her waist as she stretched up to replace one small missing stone near the top. When she set it in, the workers cheered and clapped their hands. She raised her arms in victory, then scampered down, sweating and streaked with dust. After that she was ordered to watch. Just watch.

Through her school years she told guidance counselors and college professors again and again how she was going to make the world work better. "With machines, with great inventions, we can direct floods into the deserts. We can move food to the famines and medicine to the diseased. We can cure the oil addiction by creating non-destructive energy, and build a new civilization on the bones of the old one. We can improve the quality of life; we can make people happy."

Armed with a degree from MIT and a resume printed on pearl-gray bond, she marched south through New York, Philadelphia and Washington, D.C. She did not find the fertile ground of eager intellectuals and Utopia-seekers, but a stagnant, struggling system long past caring. The cities had taken on criminal lives, consuming people, holding them hostage with dark violence. In weak defense, governments passed heavier laws and tax burdens onto its citizens. They paid lip service to quality— environmental standards, anti-discrimination, crime prevention—but it was not about making things better for people. It was about control. There were no jobs for people with dreams, especially women with dreams, when men with fat debts needed income.

Interview after interview left her cold and numb. In Washington, after a particularly long wait for a Director of Public Works who never showed up for their appointment, she got disgusted and she got drunk in her hotel bar. The Assistant Manager, a Middle-Eastern man named Anoush, intervened when she began, with animated explanation to the other guests, to take apart his espresso machine. He complimented her work and asked that she please reassemble it so they might drink some together, which they did with tiny glasses of Sambucca, until the bar closed.

The bartender turned on the lights, closed out his register and counted his tips. Roxanne looked around the room.

"It's an amazing business," she said.

"How's that?" said Anoush.

"It's all pretend. Everything. Then you turn the lights on and poof, back to reality."

"That's your reality," he said.

"What do you mean?"

"I mean," he waved his arm, "look at this. I see a carpet that needs to be vacuumed, an espresso machine with fingerprints on it, a bartender that's trying to cheat me . . ."

The bartender laughed. The boss said that every night. Anoush continued. "What do you see?"

"I see," she looked around the room. "I see a burnt-out light-bulb over there, a sign that's hanging crooked by the door. I see that if you moved those three tables into the corner you'd create a better space for the waitresses to pick up their drinks."

"Yes, that would be more organized," he said. "But it would look just that way—organized." He thought for a moment. "I want the room to feel casual, intimate. I want the people at those three tables to put their heads together and toast some special moment without waitresses stomping by with trays. I want the man to be able to see the door and the woman to be able to see her reflection in the mirror. They stay longer; they drink more in the right setting."

"Like I said, pretend."

"More than that. It's a setting. The bar, the restaurant, the rooms, the beds, the lobby. These are all settings, stage sets for people to act out their little dramas. If they're happy dramas, we have happy guests. That makes me happy. And when I'm happy, my boss is happy."

"So that's how it works."

"That's how it works, Roxanne. It's about making people happy."

"Or giving them the opportunity to be happy."

"Exactly."

"And how does *that* work?"

"Let me show you."

He escorted her through the atrium Lobby, hushed as if holding its breath, through a discreet service entrance to the place behind the scenes. This was the back of the house.

All around them, as if it were a big secret, the graveyard shift did its job. The auditors tallied the day's receipts; security walked the floors; room service collected trays; front desk clerks prepared bills for the morning departures.

He walked her past stacks of banquet chairs lined up along just-mopped, wide corridors where high racks of polished copper chafers waited for the next event. In the main kitchen, the night utility crew fed plates into the starving, steaming dishwasher as it grumbled and hissed like a toothless dragon.

"It never stops," she said.

"No, it never stops. Twenty-four hours a day, seven days a week, Christmas, New Year's. We have different calendars in this business."

He took her to his office, a neat masculine arrangement of hardwood desk and chairs, designed to make guests feel as if they were speaking to someone with authority, someone who would take care of their requests.

"This is where I sit," he said. "When I sit. But it's my job to be everywhere—or to make the staff think that I am. You can't just sit at a desk and make people happy."

She ran a hand across the polished plane of his desk. "Very nice," she said.

"Yes, very nice." He slid his hand on the wood to touch hers, then lifted it and kissed the fingertips. "And I would very much like to make you happy."

She laughed.

"I'm sorry," he said. "I thought . . ."

"Don't apologize," she said. "I didn't mean to laugh. I just never saw it coming. I mean I didn't even notice you were . . ."

"Quite all right," he said, adjusting his tie. "It's up to you." He smiled. It was genuine. "I enjoyed our tour, Roxanne." He led her congenially toward the door. "And I hope you will come and stay with us again on your next trip to the District."

"Goodnight," she said.

She fell in love that night but not with a man. She went to her room and packed her things, rode the elevator down to street level, then caught a cab for National Airport. If it was going to be the hotel business, it was going to be The Best. And that could only be one place. Back in Hawai'i, the welcoming home.

Presenting no resume or references, she applied for a job at Hale Heahea. "Let me fix something," she offered the confused Director of Engineering. With borrowed tools, she removed his desk drawer, oiled the rollers, convinced a bent runner to go back in place and tightened the knob. In the boiler room she took a reading on the water treatment and looked through the site glass at the smoky golden flame.

"You're running too rich," she told him. "If this were the city, you'd be hit with a fine on your emissions." He hired her as night supervisor, because he needed the help he said, and told her to learn fast. In six months she had his job. In two years, she was directing resort projects as Executive Assistant.

Through three owners and four management companies, she helped Hale Heahea's longstanding General Manager preserve the sense of place as best they could. During leaner economic times, she would cut corners only after serious argument, and only behind the scene where a guest would never see. Once she threatened to quit when the current efficiency experts wanted to close down one of the restaurants.

Somewhere during the last transition, the GM gave up in frustration, and she took over as General Manager, with a fierce determination to survive, to succeed, and to protect the quality. Up until this moment that is what she had done.

At exactly six A.M. there was a tap on the connecting door. It was Room Service, letting her know the coffee was on her desk. Her makeup was flawless. Roxanne walked into the office just as her cup was filled.

"Good morning, Miss Shipman," said Kaui La'au, her rotunda of a body draped in a huge pink T-shirt, flowers in her hair. "I'm sorry," she said, catching Roxanne's glance, "They took our uniforms last night."

"Thank you, Kaui," she said.

"Miss Shipman," Kaui's cow-brown eyes were mournful. "I won't be able to bring up your ten o'clock pot." Roxanne gave Kaui a kiss on the cheek.

"My dear, I shall miss you." She called upon the trained-seal smile and slipped a bill into Kaui's pocket. "I wish it could be more," she said so that Kaui wouldn't look until later and find the hundred-dollar bill.

They heard high heels click down the hall. Danielle rushed in to do her hair. As usual she was breathless and flustered, her voice opposite of her skilled, calm hands.

"You know wat—" she panted, "Everyting stay gone arready! Sucking guys tell me dey gonna move 'em first ting dis morning, but the buggahs wen took da bloody stuffs arready. I no more sharp scissahs—no more notting in da shop. Cannot even brush your hair!" She stopped. "I'm sorry, Miss Shipman."

"You know—" said Roxanne. "Dose boys gonna get dirty lickins, 'cause da boss stay plenny piss off wen she get one bad hair day!" They laughed together, surprised at themselves, out of context. "I'll see you at the new shop when you're set up," she said. "I'll be your first customer."

"I hate it," Danielle said. "I just hate it."

The phone rang. Kaui and Danielle scurried back into the day. She answered.

"Roxanne."

Him. She clung to the voice on the phone. Rich in tone, it projected images of purple orchids and honey, bassoon music, thunder. Never suggestive, the passion was erotic in a different way, intense and clean.

"I was thinking you might call," she said. "I was hoping you would."

"How are you?"

"Fine. Rotten. You know. It's hard."

"I know."

The phone grew warmer, such *mana* coming through the lines. She inhaled deeply, feeling strength surround her like a glittering fog. She covered the receiver with her hand so he would not hear her gasp, resting against the chair's leather chest, gripping its left forearm in her fingers.

"I'm on auto-pilot, I guess. I keep wondering when I'm going to feel something."

"You're doing well."

"I'm not doing anything. That's the worst of it. There's nothing I can do to stop this. They're closing us down. We're closing. That's that."

"It's not your fault."

"I know but . . ." She closed her eyes, tried as always to imagine the face behind the voice. "I keep thinking there must be something I could do, should do, should have done."

"There's nothing. You aren't supposed to do anything. Be yourself."

"Talk to me," she said and took a deep breath. "Say anything."

He talked. The words were not as important as the quality of the voice. It poured strength into her. She felt it enter, felt the tension drain out. "I watched them yesterday," he said. "The new owners. They walked around looking at everything that way, like they owned it. Like they even owned the staff. It was sickening. The staff did their job and smiled. They're still smiling. You trained them well. You should be very proud. I'm proud of you."

"Thank you," she said.

"The place looks wonderful. The *wiliwili* trees are blooming. Did you notice? And they're full of birds, the little green mejiro that flit around all day like they're just happy to be alive. The beach is perfect, pristine-clean and not a cloud in the sky. The golf course looks like it's making a living being green."

She listened to him talk. Sometimes it reminded her of Anoush's voice, a voice with authority but without the accent. She remembered the first time he called. It was right after she'd arrived at Hale Heahea.

"Roxanne," he said.

"Yes?"

"Welcome home."

"Who's calling, please?"

"Your biggest fan."

"I beg your pardon?"

"I'm glad you're here."

That was it. Then a few days later he called again. It always started with her name.

"Roxanne."

"Who are you and why are you calling me?"

"It doesn't matter and because you need to hear my voice."

"It matters to me. What do you want? What is your name? How do you know me?"

He never answered her questions. Instead he would distract her from himself with talk about work. Sometimes he would distract her from work with talk about music or books. Often, he made her laugh.

She never knew who he was; she never told anyone about the calls. She never told him how important they were to her, but he must have known because he never stopped. He called pre-disaster or post-celebration with encouragement or congratulations. He called in the middle of a hurricane watch and sounded like the eye of the storm. He called the day her father died, and the morning she first sat at the General Manager's desk.

And what he said at the beginning was true; she needed to hear his voice. Especially today.

"I would like to have a number where I can reach you," he said. "After today."

"I don't know what it will be."

"Let me know when you do."

"How?"

He didn't answer. "It's going to be OK," he said.

"I know." *Now*, she thought, *now I can mourn*. But the call ended and she was left without the voice, without tears. She looked out the window at the beach.

She poured more coffee, closed her eyes and enjoyed the smell before the sip. The call, the chair, the coffee, the ocean. *Somehow we're going to get through this together.* Another deep breath.

It was time to start handling the next twelve hours, until the final ceremony. She walked out of the office with a smile on her face, feeling light, as one feels at the funeral after an expected death, distant and calm.

It was still early. There were no guests, of course. They had all checked out yesterday, leaving literally hundreds of stories, hundreds of human moments commemorated here. They begged her not to change anything, as if changing the physical body of the place would somehow change their memories.

"I recovered from three different major surgeries here. It's part of my healing."

"Where do we go now? My children have never spent Christmas anywhere else."

"This was my grandfather's favorite place on earth. We scattered his ashes there, in the ocean just off that point."

"I got married here—three times!"

"It's the only place that never changes. When we're here, when we walk on the same beach, when we have the same breakfast at the same table, we're still young. It's still us from years ago. Do you understand? We're happy again."

She would remember them all, but consciously refused to carry them around with her, a knapsack full of obligations—memories to protect. There was work to be done. To herself, she had only one obligation; once fulfilled the others would be satisfied. Quality must be preserved. At whatever cost.

She walked through the empty lobby and down to a small terrace overlooking the brilliant ocean. The terrace was set inconspicuously behind a rock wall, a subtle round mosaic with radiating spokes of granite slab. She believed this was the center, the *piko*, of Hale Heahea. She stood there on the warm tile, enjoying the familiar offshore breeze, drawing strength from this moment before, as all other moments would soon be after.

Does everything have to change? Does quality?

As with many priceless things in a deteriorating society, Hale Heahea had been sold once and then again, and every turnover was a step downward. Then earthquakes and unprecedented fires in California cut the heartline of their main market. A war somewhere in the world frightened older travelers. The struggling airlines trimmed flights to Hawai'i and put on larger, more crowded planes. When mainland economy began to fail in earnest, the travel industry could barely comprehend, much less take action. By then hardly anyone could afford the prestige and respite of luxury travel.

Finally, a Japanese company bought Hale Heahea. Fear of change immediately drove away another percentage of the occupancy; unavoidable decline accelerated. The loss of quality was most subtle and most horrifying. Quality requires accountability, and is not relative. When the new team came in, with its mini computers and marathon consensus meetings, quality began to sneak away like the moon in the morning.

In desperation Hale Heahea lowered prices, made exceptions to its lofty rules, made cut-backs in staffing for the first time. And for the first time in its history, Hale Heahea—the welcoming home—no longer greeted arriving guests at the front door with a *lei*.

Abruptly, she stopped thinking. She put the thoughts away in a particular drawer in her mind, and turned to witness the closing. It was like a war or a hurricane. Groundskeepers marched through the gardens with picks and shovels, digging up plants, draining ponds. Housemen passed down corridors, stripped art off the walls; raided the guest rooms for sheets and towels and finally furniture. They dumped laundry at the loading dock where it waited for trucks like a pile of bodies, reaching the ceiling, reeking of mold and dying.

Like captured slaves, people who worked there most of their lives loaded boxes and disconnected computers, walked with blank faces past the deserted lobby, the vacant beach, the butchered kitchens, through cleaning crews packing up pots and pans, wiping out walk-ins, robbing pantry shelves.

In spite of all the endless plans, managers were unprepared for this. In spite of all the pieces of paper they had to explain and justify, they sat at their desks and looked out their windows, fingering receivers of dead telephones, stroking the polished wood planes of desks.

As an area was pronounced clear, the members of the staff left *lei*. They draped the front desk with them. They hung them on the doorknobs and cash registers. They laid them over the giant sandstone hands of the Buddha. They piled them on Roxanne's shoulders in a flower pillar up to her eyebrows. She carried them all, all day.

When she went down to Engineering, she watched Cedric Takamoto, with tears in his eyes, turn in his tools in a cardboard box, their old metal bones shiny with WD-40. He had brought her an orchid from his yard, a remarkable thing the color of mulled wine. She held it in her hand and told him to keep the tools. He refused; it wouldn't be fair to the other guys.

It would be hard to think of Hale Heahea without Cedric. He had gone into closets and corners, mechanical rooms and pumphouses, deep in the cores of machinery and high on the roofs of elevators, tinkering, tightening, tuning and talking to every part. He would retire before they re-opened. Who would know where the shut-off valves for the irrigation system were? Who would pick the lock on Reefer #1, when the cook took the key home? Then she remembered. It didn't matter.

The new managers emptied the place. All the beautiful, heirloom things were loaded up and shipped out to another property on another island. "For safekeeping," they said. "During construction. Everything will be returned to its proper place." *When?* she thought. *How do you know what's proper? Do you have any idea what you're doing?*

She watched the trucks pull out all day, slowly draining the life from the place, while the new managers ran around with clipboards as if they were guns, pointing them at trucks, pointing them at her people. She felt their humiliation. She wanted to close the gate and not let any more trucks out. She wanted to tell them to stop—don't help them; don't make it easy on them. She wished she had a hand grenade. It would have done less damage.

The day continued unstoppable. At five o'clock, it was time to get ready for the ceremony. She ran through the office to change clothes but the shock of its emptiness stopped her. The telephone, alone on the floor, was all that remained in the barren room. She was paralyzed by the void and suddenly terrified. "Ring," she commanded the phone, and it stupidly did not. Everything was gone. The chair was gone.

Suddenly exhausted, she removed the rings of *lei* and held them in her hands. There was no place to hang them. She couldn't put them on the floor.

"Roxanne."

Frozen, trying to breathe through the block ice the air had become, she heard the familiar voice from far away. "Roxanne." She could not move. He approached her from behind, his chest filling the space that was the chair's space, his shoulders there. He reached forward, palms raised, lifting her limp hands full of flowers. He held her arms with his two, strong as the wooden arms of the chair. She breathed; they breathed together. "Don't turn around," he said, "unless you're ready to leave with me."

"What do you want?"

"We only have a moment. Listen. Once Hale Heahea closes, I can't come back."

"Why?"

"There's no reason for me to. Listen . . ." He held her, very still. She concentrated on the moment, trying not to think, to question. "I work here. I'm your employee. My job is over and I'm going elsewhere. None of us are allowed back through the gate; they've made that clear. I want you to come with me. I have a place for you."

"A place to stay?"

"No. A place to live, where you can do the work you were born to do."

"Where?"

"I can't tell you. It's very special, like your hotel here. And you have to be very special to be there. A group of us, my friends— we dreamed it; we created it, and we defend it. As you would, as you have, Hale Heahea."

"Who are you?"

"You don't know me, but I have known you for a long, long time. I watched you grow from a little girl into a beautiful woman. I watched you go away to school and I watched you come back, as I knew you would. We want you with us, and I . . ." She felt the shudder run through him and struggled to turn around and look at his face, but he held her fast.

"Let me think about it. I have to go to the ceremony now. Please let me go."

"Don't. Don't make this easier on them. Let them explain to the press how Roxanne Shipman refused to be part of their PR parade."

"It needs to be done properly," she said, "Hale Heahea deserves that."

"Hale Heahea is destroyed," he said. "You know it. You know it can never be the same."

"No," she said quietly, "I don't. Those of us who stay behind, and remember, have to protect it for the ones who leave."

"You are so strong—and so wrong." He folded her *lei* and his arms around her, as the current of energy passed through them both. She would turn now. She would turn and see his face. They would embrace, and all the agonizing time alone would slowly drown, replacing pain with love, and questioning with faith.

"You make people happy," he said. "It's a gift."

"It's more than happiness," she said. "It's—"

"Miss Shipman!" Danielle called as she approached. "Everybody stay waiting for you!" He was gone like a hallucination. And Roxanne Shipman, General Manager, rushed toward Danielle.

"Help me find my things!" she said. They tore through her bedroom, fortunately still intact. The chair was there, in a corner; the *pu'olo* sat in its seat. Danielle grabbed her steel gray *holoku*, the color of sky over ocean on a stormy day. She opened the *pu'olo* and tossed the jade and crown flower *lei* around Roxanne's neck as they ran to the lobby.

She stood with the others in front of the hotel, scanning the crowd, wondering if he was there watching her. When the time came she stooped over the long *maile lei* and watched her own hands take the two ends of it. She felt like an old, old woman as she stared at the *maile* in her fingers while Kahu spoke the words. She wished with all her heart that the magic could be true, that these green leaves picked in the mountains for centuries by the appointed, could indeed protect Hale Heahea from evil, could lead the way to cleansing and rebirth.

Her hands, without understanding, tied the ends together, and although the hands were deaf to the blessing falling on them they responded to some instruction from her brain and did the work. The crowd of curious pressed in close to see it; cameras clicked and buzzed like swarms of beetles; women sniffed into tissues and men looked at the ground. Kahu, his white robes blazing in the hot sun, dipped the *ti* leaf into his *koa* bowl, the one handed down from Kamehameha the Great, and sprinkled water into the sunshine, blessing, blessing endlessly. The heat, the growing brightness, the words after words, the people, faces blurred and unfamiliar, seemed to steal the air from the place and for a moment she felt panic surge up. She wanted to run, to run to him and let him take her in his arms again and make this go away.

When it was finally done, and the band played "Hawai'i Aloha," she walked regally down the path to the little *piko* look-out. They all followed. She stood a moment, then removed the beautiful *lei* and held it firmly. "People say," she recited, "that if you throw your *lei* into the ocean, and it washes back to shore, you are promised to return." She folded the flowers back and forth in her hands while the cameras set up and the sun cooperated into position. She then, dramatically as planned, turned and tossed the jade and crown flowers into the water, thinking *just come back*. The others' flowers followed hers, and the waves received them graciously. Soon, as if themselves rehearsed, the *lei* lined up in a rip current headed out to sea, one after another, a chain of hopes, unlinked.

She managed to turn on the automatic hostess in her brain, accepted kind words and goodbyes, the smiling and posing, the toasting with champagne. Inside, her soul's eye focused on the pretty queue of departing *lei*, until at some point she realized that everyone was leaving and she would be gratefully alone. The wind was starting to change and the tide was going out. After the last tearful employee had gone, she followed the stone path to the beach, where two beach chairs with broken slats had been left behind, along with two empty beer bottles. She wondered who had salvaged them for one last sunset toast, and made a mental note to speak to the Food & Beverage Director. Then she remembered.

When she sat down, she was finally aware of how tired she was. She kicked off her shoes, put her feet up. "I'm just going to watch for a while," she said to a bothered sand crab, hurrying into the surf. She looked out at the *lei* again, watching until she could no longer make out the last one drifting away, fading in the finally fading light, and drifted herself, to sleep.

"Roxanne."

She woke up at once. It was so dark. *What happened to the torches?* Oh.

"Roxanne."

"I can't see you," she said.

"When was the last time you ate?"

She laughed, "I don't know."

"Here, I've brought us something. Have some coffee."

"Wonderful," she said. *How does he know?*

Perfect coffee in a thermos, still-warm homemade bread, a heavenly mango he sliced to share with her. She studied him in the moonglow. He was large for the chair, wide-shouldered. He had on a shirt with the sleeves rolled up. She couldn't see his eyes. She watched the movement of his hands with the knife on the mango. They were good hands.

He talked. "The ceremony was beautiful. I don't know if anybody was listening to Kahu's words, but he obviously worked hard on saying exactly the right thing. He talked about preserving tradition, but he also talked about moving forward. Did you notice? Allowing the place to change." He cut a piece of mango and held it on the knife edge, lifted it up to her mouth. She ate it; it was delicious.

She said, "Change. I've heard so much about change in the last few weeks it makes me sick. We go to all this trouble, all these years of establishing ourselves as the best in the business, the best in the world. Preaching high-minded attitudes about stewardship and aloha to the staff. And now we have to change—change for economic reasons. It's not about quality. It never was."

He slipped her another slice of mango. "Are you sure?" he said.

She sipped the coffee, then passed the cup to him. "I don't know. You put your heart and soul into something. Not just me, many people's hearts and souls for years—and it just goes away. It's sold. For money. Like a used car. It's not right, not morally right. Some places are better. They deserve better."

"You're right," he said. "Some places are. Some people are. Have you thought about what you're going to do?"

"No," she said. "Yes." She paused for a long time. He wiped the knife blade across the knee of his jeans.

"Why don't you take some time—get away from here for a while?"

"I've thought about that," she said. "They want me to stay on, take an office in town and 'maintain community relations.' They say they're going to re-open when they have the money to renovate the building. A year, maybe two. I don't know."

"You don't have to."

"Don't I?"

He finished the mango; walked down to the ocean, bent and rinsed his hands. His hair was long, tied back. It was crackled with silver. When he turned to come back, she saw he had a short beard. He smiled. She could see it in the dark. *He said he was an employee. We don't allow long hair and beards. Who is this man?*

The night was remarkably still and clear. Without the hotel's lights to hide them, bright stars stretched across the sky like a reflection of the beach, as many as grains of sand.

"Your whole life," he said. "You've been working for huge things—grand ideals, quality. Did it ever occur to you that you didn't have to do that? Did it ever occur to you that you can do something, work, for yourself?"

"I *do* do this for myself. I happen to like huge things." She laughed. It altered the moment.

"I told you I have a place. It's not huge, but it's huge in value, to us. It's on the other side of the island, at the bottom of what used to be a sugar cane plantation. We managed to get the money together a few years ago, and now we are almost completely self-sufficient. We still have to work elsewhere for money—or other reasons." He looked at her, then continued as if he had changed his mind about what he was going to say. "We farm; we fish; we make things we need. You'd be amazed how the quality of your life changes when your whole goal is just to live it. Live it well. Happily."

"I can't imagine that."

"Yes you can. Think about it. You choose the people you want around you. Not small-minded people with small ideas—huge-minded people with huge ideas. People with passion. You let them do what they want to do—write, paint, plant. You let them build windmills or statues, conduct music or electricity, raise children or genetically engineered vegetables. People want to do what they have passion for. We let them."

"Sounds too good to be true," she said. "Sounds like a cult."

"A cult is built around one charismatic leader. We don't have that. Unless you count Thomas Jefferson."

"What has he got to do with it?'

"Life, liberty and the pursuit of happiness," he said. "That's all there is to it. That's all there ever was. It's not about money. It's about this. We found a way to make it work. Well." She could hear the smile in his voice. He was proud of the place. It meant a great deal to him. As she did. *Why?*

"I wouldn't mind trying a life like that. And I have nowhere to go. But I would have to come back to the real world eventually."

"No," he said. "That's what you have to understand. You can come back if you want to, but this is not the real world. Reality is not like this—forced on you by other people's demands. It's yours. You own it. You have a mind and a heart. You have gifts. We can give you the place, the resources, the time to develop them."

"Everyone has gifts."

He shook his head. "Think about the people you work for. Their lives are only built at the expense of others, and their reality is only borrowed from what others tell them. They cannot possibly understand the value of themselves. They cannot possibly understand the quality."

"I do. And I promised to bring it back."

"You can't. There is nothing left here. The only way for you is with me, and I promise too, that you will find what you're looking for."

"That," she said, laughing, "by your own definition, is *your* reality."

He laughed. She had caught him in his own web. She liked making him laugh. She liked hearing it on the telephone; she liked seeing it even more. It made her feel light and alive.

"Who are you?" she asked.

"Why do you always have to ask questions? Why can't you just accept this and go with it. You want to. I know you do."

"I want to know."

"I'm the ghost of Christmas past. I'm Prince Charming with your glass slipper in the trunk of my car. I'm Rhett Butler, Humphrey Bogart and Spencer Tracy. I'm your *'aumakua*, your father's spirit watching over you. I'm every man you ever turned away because you were too busy to admit what you really wanted. I'm the genie in the bottle. I'm your biggest fan. I know who you really are and I want you to be with me. Is that good enough?"

She opened her mouth but words would not come out. She stood. She wanted to run. He took her in his arms. He said, "It's up to you."

Daylight caught her sleeping in the beach chair, his shirt spread across her chest. She opened her eyes and looked at the pink ocean. She sat up and stretched, then stood and untwisted her dress, wrapped his shirt around her shoulders. The sand was cool on her feet. The tide was coming in. The highwater mark drew a shiny line one step in front of her. Then she saw it.

A heap of beach debris, wet, crushed and sandy. The most beautiful thing she had ever seen in her life. The jade and crown flower *lei*. She cheered aloud, picked it up and threw it around her neck. Seawater splattered the gray *holoku*. His shirt fell off, as she danced around a circle in the wet sand.

A magnificent wave crashed. She looked down the coastline, watching it break all the way to the end. There were footprints on the shore, somehow in a pattern of straight lines. *Letters?* She could not see them all. *What does it say?* She started to walk, then faster, then ran to beat the onrushing waves to the answer, ƎИИАХОЯ АНОⱢА.

My name reflected. She wondered if she would hear the voice again, saying her name. She wondered if it had been real, if he had been a real man or some part of herself she dreamed up—to give her the strength to do what she had to do.

It's for the best. The way everything in my life has been. For The Best.

She started toward the stone path that led back up to the hotel. Another wave boomed behind her. She turned around and saw the ocean begin to wash the bottom of the letters. Something caught her eye.

The shirt. A wave was slipping it off the sand; tugging it out to sea. She watched it go.

Then something called her, a voice deep inside, something

she could no longer ignore or refuse. *No.* She ran; splashed waist-deep into the ocean, her heavy dress dragging her back. The shirt floated out like a swimmer in trouble, just out of reach. She dove for it. And won.

Soaked and sandy, weaving in the glittering surf, she dug into the pocket where she knew it had to be. It was wet but not illegible.

The map.

Now, she thought. *Now it's up to me.*

There was always a breeze through Hale Heahea, the welcoming home. This morning it whispered through empty hallways, ruffling *lei* draped across the front desk and scattering petals down wide stone staircases. It brushed an orchid across the *piko* of the place, then dropped down onto the beach, to chill then dry the steel gray *holoku* draped across a broken beach chair.

The General Manager was taking a swim. It was the right place to be, at the right time.

 REALITY'S TITS

It's August, the day after my forty-third birthday, and I have procrastinated long enough. I have heard the usual horror stories about women who wait. I have a brother back on the mainland in public relations for the American Cancer Society. It's time to be grown up and in control of my own well being as a woman. I'm going to schedule a mammogram.

I work up to it with softer procedures. I get my hair colored-for the first time (which any woman who's starting to gray will agree is a health issue.) Next, I get my teeth fixed, and then have a couple of questionable moles removed.

Courageous now, I call my doctor. He writes an order for the mammogram. I announce to all my friends at work that it is arranged for Friday.

When the day comes, I am feeling very brave. I am dressed for the office and prepared for some waiting with a good book. I step into the lobby of the island's brand-new hospital for the first time. There is my neighbor, Mrs. Nakagawa, who is a senior citizen volunteer at Reception, and Mr. Loo who planted the gardens. They greet me like a daughter and walk me down a long, sunny hall to Registration. So far, so good.

At Registration, the woman asks me if this is my first time. I tell her yes, with confidence.

She nods, says, "You'll be OK." She then goes into a seven-or eight-minute history of her own mammography, subsequent breast cancer and mastectomy, whereafter I could only stare at her breasts. "This one," she says, pointing with some pride to the right.

From Registration I proceed down endless and less sunny corridors to Radiology, where I run into someone else I know, a woman who used to work as a secretary at the hotel. She looks great and we exchange hugs and the usual family inquiries.

"What's wrong?" she asks.

"Nothing." I must have given her a blank look.

"You're in the hospital," she says helpfully.

(Oh, of course.) "Mammogram," I say.

"Good girl," she says, "Is this your first time?"

"Yes."

"Oh." She says, "It's not that bad."

Great. She takes me around a corner to Radiology, where I briefly balk and ask for the ladies room.

"There's one right here," she says. "You take care now. I gotta run." She leaves me at a unisex ADA restroom big enough for two paraplegic Sumos to wrestle in. I study the mirror. I have on makeup. My face resembles something like self-assurance, and after all I've come this far. I shall face Radiology. How bad could it be?

Radiology is a too-nice room full of toys, with a TV and a little window into a storage area. Inside are racks of rotating files on a motorized thing like you see at the dry cleaners. I have to wonder why it couldn't be that simple—just have your file dry cleaned every year after you're forty. Or is it every six months?

Another woman asks me if this is my first time and says it won't be that bad. She gives me more papers to fill out. Every paper asks the first day of my last period. I wonder if this is a test.

If you lie about your menstrual cycle are you likely to lie about self-examination? Are you more like to have cancer if you're a liar, and do you go on the bottom of the list for treatment if you are?

There is soap opera on the TV, with at least a hard R-rating. Half a dozen older women are watching carefully. Their children, or grandchildren, are playing with a xylophone and other stuff on the floor. I wonder if all the ladies are here for mammograms or if they just drop by this particular waiting room to watch this particular daytime drama.

I try to read my book, but I can't take my eyes off the seduction on TV. Jeff has Cynthia on the couch and she is down to bra and half slip, black of course. The smacking of their kisses is so loud it sounds like a *li hing mui* contest for the deaf. His hand is almost on her breast. Suddenly, there is a knock at the door.

"Catherine?"

I jump up. "Oh. Yes." I give my semi-confident smile and follow still another woman, who asks me if this is my first time, through a door marked Mammography. I don't remember being asked this question so much when I lost my virginity.

"Take off your blouse and your bra and put this on (a nice cotton wrap instead of the paper gown). Someone will be with you in a moment."

I am surprised at the room's pleasantness. It is small and cozy. There are murals of dolphins and tropical flowers painted on the walls, donated by local artists to the hospital. There are a couple of chairs and a desk with a lamp. Someone has draped a scarf over the lampshade so the room is softly lit. Ambience.

I'm trying to ignore the machine.

The room is nice and warm. I get changed and hang my things on a convenient hook. They've thought of everything.

The technician comes in. She actually reads the chart and

says, "Oh, this is your first time." She is kind, dressed in pink. Her nametag is decorated with stickers. Hearts, angels, that sort of thing. I read her tag because somebody I work with's wife is supposed to be a technician here. It isn't her name; no extra chitchat is required. "It's not so bad," she says, leading me over to the corner where the machine looms like some sadistic exercise equipment. It says SIEMANS.

"Don't they make air compressors?" I ask. She laughs. She opens my gown, removes my left breast like a leftover chicken and places it on the cold plate of the machine. She puts one of my hands on a handle, has me hold the gown back with the other. She tells me to put my chin here and my shoulder there. Then she crawls under me and reaches around from underneath to adjust me some more.

I can't believe the awkwardness of this machine. A man must have been designed it. No question. Siemans, I keep thinking. How much compression does it actually take to flatten your common mammary?

"I'm going to start squeezing now," she says. "As soon as we have the picture, the machine will release. Don't move and don't breathe until it does."

I brace for excruciating pain, which never comes. I stifle a laugh. Here I am with my tit in the literal wringer, in this silly room with the girlie ambience. Here's this busy little woman buzzing around me like a nervous waitress. Then she clicks over the computer and bingo, no worse than dental x-rays. OK, hold your breath. OK, hold this. OK, other side. Thank you ma'am. Nothing to it.

"That's it?" I ask.

"That's it," she says. I am surprised how easy it is. I leave the hospital whistling. Mammogram. Big deal. I feel so good I go to work and tell everyone they should sign up. Why, I had added years to my life today. I had accomplished a great thing, conquered my fear. That was it. It was done. That was Friday.

My husband and I have a great weekend. We go for drinks and listen to Ho'oku Street Band at the Clubhouse on Friday. We trim the bougainvillea and go to the dump on Saturday. I clean out the birdcage. On Sunday I wash my car, and then make chili and rice for friends who come over to watch "Star Trek."

Late in the day I call my office voice mail. One message is from the hospital. "Please call right away." What? Oh, the mammogram results, the all clear. Sure, I'll call in the morning.

On Monday, I go to the office. I get my coffee, open the mail and update the calendars. I look at the morning reports. I take a few phone messages, and then I get the second call from the nurse. Yes, there is something the radiologist wants to take another look at. Yes, we need to schedule another appointment. No, it's nothing to worry about yet. (Yet.) Yes, she would fax me a copy of the report. Yes, Thursday would be fine.

Uh oh.

The fax comes through and it is a full page of words. The only seven I can read are "eight millimeter mass in the right breast."

Uh oh.

A tiny dark feeling begins coming towards me from far away, galaxies away. It would take time to get here, but it is approaching like an eight-millimeter meteorite to impact on the surface of my life. I am at the office so I let the business mind work through the day, reassuring the rest of my brain with thoughts of good health insurance and the brand new hospital, thoughts of time off and books to read. I read the fax again. "No cause for concern" is somewhere in there. I decide to go with that.

At home I sit outside and drink a beer, waiting for my husband to come home. It is another beautiful evening, another beautiful sunset. He is right on time and joins me. We sit for a while and he tells me about the things he fixed today, a joke he heard.

"How big is eight millimeters?" I ask. He looks at me directly, not asking why. I can see the inventory running through his amazing brain. He holds up one finger, then thinks of something and goes into the back of the garage. While he rummages around, I go upstairs for two more beers. When I come back down he is holding a little socket wrench.

"This is eight millimeters," he says, and gives it to me. It is bigger than I thought it would be, the size of a pencil eraser, the size of a green pea. I look through the open socket at his face.

"I have to get more X-rays," I tell him. "The radiologist sees something eight millimeters in my right breast."

"It's nothing," he says. And that's it.

I believe in thinking positive. I don't believe in worrying until it's necessary. I don't believe in working through all the fatal possibilities and listening to everybody's horror stories. I decide to deal with this privately for that reason and go alone again to the next set of x-rays on the following Thursday. I fill out another set of papers. I put down the first day of my last period again. I visit with Jeff and Cynthia again, this time on the balcony of a lighthouse, kissing like starving leeches.

"Catherine?"

Same cute room, same Siemans equipment. But I'm an old

pro now, and I get undressed as instructed and study the dolphins on the wall again and read a pamphlet about treatment options with the early detection of breast cancers. This time when the technician comes, she is my coworker's wife. So we are now required to make small talk about work and so forth and what a pleasure to meet you. I feel bad for her, having to be known by so many nervous women coming in here to have their breasts squeezed by her machine and then, well, and then they have to chat.

She is very nice. We face the machine together. She studies the previous x-rays and says excuse me while she takes my breast and rolls it onto the glass plate. She compresses. It's not bad. She releases, then prints out and looks at the shot. Nothing there. I breathe a sigh of relief. She does it again. Nothing. I am convinced that the first series of pictures was a mistake. She works and works on the computer. She moves my arm and crawls around me. She flattens my breast with her hand and rolls it like *sushi*.

"There it is," she says, "That's it." Damn. She takes another picture just to be sure. "Please stay undressed while I show these to the radiologist. He may want me to get some more while I have you here." I wait. Yes, he does want more, so we try again. This time she shows me what my eight-millimeter looks like, which I have been trying and trying to feel, but it must be deep inside and I can't even believe it, but there it is on the film.

"OK," she says sweetly, "You can get dressed now. That's it."

"That's it?" I ask. What must the look on my face have said? That's it I have breast cancer or that's it I don't, or that's it I have to wait some more, or that's it the doctor will see you now?

"That's it." She says it with a smile and she gives me a hug. This does not make me feel better. "If you don't get the results in a few days, I'd give them a call."

I get dressed. I go to the desk at Radiology. I ask if they need a payment today. "No, that's it," they say.

That's it.

I do not get the results in a couple of days. Another weekend passes. I call the hospital on Monday and someone says they'll call me back. My doctor calls me back instead. I have not talked to him since this whole thing started, but I have come to hate him by now. This is, after all, his fault. He sent me.

His voice is overly friendly. Yes, there is something there and the radiologist is recommending a sonogram.

"Why didn't they do that in the first place?" I ask.

"Well, that's a good question," he says. "It's a test that can rule out certain things. Chances are that the mass is a benign cyst, as most breast lumps are, eighty percent or so, but the sonogram will show that. If a cyst is not indicated, then we can pursue other diagnostics. It's a process of elimination."

"So if it's a cyst, the sonogram will show that," I say.

"Right," he says.

"And if it's not?" I ask.

"Well then we can talk about your options. There are a lot of treatment options with breast lumps. People don't usually think of it that way, but there are. It may be something to just keep an eye on, or we may want to do a biopsy now. Or you may want to consult with a surgeon."

"What's involved with the biopsy?"

"Well, we'll insert a long needle into the lump for a sample of tissue which we'll send to the lab for the biopsy."

"A long needle?"

"We'll use a local anesthetic," he says. "Well, any other questions?"

"Yes. What else is there?"

"I'm sorry?"

"What else is there on the menu? You said there were lots of treatment options."

"Well, we've pretty much covered it. We could do a lumpectomy if you're really worried about it. We could just go in and take it out," the doctor explains.

"Let's do that," I say.

"Well," he says again. He says that a lot. "Well, you don't want to undergo any unnecessary procedures."

Like a lot of tests with expensive equipment? Like a sonogram? I'm thinking this but I don't say it. Instead I say, "Thank you."

I make an appointment for the sonogram, or ultra-sound. Now it will be a committee, Cathey's Tit Committee. Hell, they don't even look like mine anymore. They aren't mine. Mine have been perfect all these years. These are Reality's tits. And Reality's tits are going to require some work.

Days go by. I go to work, I go home. The routine goes on and I try not to think of it. It's not really scary yet. I'm not making any deals with God. Breast cancer. Tragic. I imagine buying all new clothes, getting a few tattoos. And when I go bald during radiation I would have a picture made in "Star Trek" costume and pointy ears, to go on the back of my memoirs.

At some point, maybe over the weekend, I have a conversation with a girlfriend and tell her about the sonogram. "I'll go with you," she says.

"No, no, that's not necessary," I say at once. She has children. She has a part time job and a mother-in-law to take care of. I would need her more, later.

"You don't understand Cathey," she says. "I love to go to the doctor. It gets me out of the house."

"OK. September 21st. Can I buy you lunch?"

"It's a date. Now that's the first day of fall," she says. "Let's wear autumn colors."

We meet at the restaurant and eat sandwiches and drink a beer for lunch. Why not? We compare notes on x-rays and mammograms and compliment each other's earth-tone outfits. She says if I had to have more tests, we could have lunch every week.

She has worn mismatched earrings to make me laugh, and they do. "I brought you something to help make you well," she says. "It's a Japanese mushroom from my mother-in-law. She and her friends make a tonic from it." She hands me a Tupperware container and sheet of instructions on how to take care of it. "Don't open it. It stinks," she says.

It looks like a giant wad of gray chewing gum. "What do I do with it?"

"Read the instructions," she says. "You have to give it black tea everyday and you have to name it one of the names on this list, and you can't let it die until it has a baby. Then you peel the baby off and throw the mother away, but then you have to give the baby a name."

I look at her dubiously. "Does it help?"

"I have no idea," she says. "It probably died in the car." We laugh until it's time to go pick up my X-rays.

At Radiology, my friend checks out the soap opera while the technician hands me a large manila envelope with the word "Mammography" printed on the front, and a discreet diagram of a giant naked boob on the back.

We go down another endless hall to where the sonogram machine is, of course, in Maternity. Somebody is having a baby, and we have to wait longer, so we go for coffee. We run into a lady we know, waiting for her great-granddaughter to be born. The whole family has shown up. They are laughing, drinking sodas and bragging like it's a party. When they get word that the baby is coming, everybody leaves in high spirits.

Finally it's time for me to go in, and my friend has to leave. I can't thank her enough and she says to call her when I have to come again. Even if I don't need any more tests, she'll tell her husband I have some mysterious condition so we can have lunch every week. She makes me laugh again. It is a blessing.

The sonogram room is a dark walk-in closet compared to the muted ambience of Mammography. Boxes are stacked in all the corners. A cot is set up next to a computer terminal with a large color monitor and double-size keyboard. At least there are no mashing or squeezing parts.

A very young man in lab coat greets me by saying "Ready?" He has a toothpick in his mouth. "Come on in." There is an even younger girl with him, also in lab coat. She takes me behind a curtain, asks me to remove everything from the waist up, put on the gown and lie down next to the sonogram machine. I leave my clothes on some of the boxes. So much for the convenient hook.

The girl turns the lights down even more, and the toothpick man sits at the machine while she hovers behind him. He is practically jovial as he picks up a huge tube of something like KY jelly and squeezes a cold glob onto the right tit. He takes a thing like a computer mouse and rolls it over, under, all around the breast.

I watch the nipple grow ridiculously tall, and decide not to be embarrassed by it. It doesn't belong to me, after all. It's Reality's tit.

The man is watching too.

"Can I see the monitor?" I ask, diverting our attention.

"Sure." He turns the screen around and shows me the inside of the tit on TV. It looks like the ocean when you fly over, wavy, blue-white and uncertain.

"Looks like a music video," I say. He laughs.

"I can make it change colors," and he does. It goes through a whole spectrum of cloudy, bubbly images from Day-glo chartreuse to gray on gray. We talk about what kind of music would go with it, and if he entered it into a contest, who would ever figure out what it really was. I am just about to break into "Smoke on the Water" in front of the mortified girl, when he pauses on an orange-umber screen. "This one matches your skirt," he says, and prints it out for me.

"Can I keep this?" I ask. Reality's tit, I'm thinking, in her autumn colors.

"Sure," he says. Then he apparently remembers that he shouldn't be playing with the equipment. He puts on more jelly, rolls the mouse some more. He turns to the girl, more than a little frustrated. "If it's eight millimeters, I should be able to find it like that!" snapping his fingers. He rolls the mouse over and over. He squeezes the tit and pushes it over. He rolls and presses and rolls. I think he's starting to sweat.

I am feeling both annoyed and elated. This is taking way too long, but he can't find anything. That's a good thing, right?

"So it went away?" I ask.

"Uh," he says, "I need to go talk with the radiologist. Stay right here." He leaves me with the girl. I stare at the ceiling. She tries to be nice.

"Do you have to go back to work this afternoon?" she asks.

"No."

Finally the two guys come in and she backs into a corner. The radiologist stands at my feet, me still lying on my back with the tit hanging out. He does a fifteen-minute take on breast lumps and tests for same, and the reason that cysts don't show up on sonograms.

"Oh," I say. "So this is not a good thing?" My mood is rapidly solidifying.

"All this indicates is that the mass is not a cyst, and that you should consult with your doctor about further options. I will write this in your record and share it with him."

Options again. Like a new Winnebago. Did you want the rear seat air bags with that? No thanks, just leave me one in front.

I don't understand what he's trying to tell me. If there's nothing there, that should be good. But if there's something there that didn't show up, that's bad. Either way, I want to ask him why I have to make another appointment to hear it from somebody else. Instead I say "Thank you."

He leaves. The girl leaves. The toothpick guy, like a finished lover, flips my gown back over the tit and says, "I'm sure it's OK, like you said. It was a cyst and it went away."

"Yeah right."

More days. Another weekend. More phone calls. I talk with the doctor on the phone and I tell him I don't want to fool around. I want the lump removed. I feel very feminist and in control when I say this. "I'm with you," he says. "I feel we should always lead breast lumps rather than follow them." I wonder if he leads or follows when he dances, and what dance exactly a doctor does with a breast lump. Certainly not the tango; it takes two.

He refers me to a surgeon. I make another appointment and another lunch date with my girlfriend.

Weeks have gone by since this started, I keep thinking. Weeks in which this cancer, if it is, could be growing and getting worse. I am losing my sense of humor and I am losing my faith in the health education I have had from "Cosmopolitan." I am wondering why doctors are too young, why they don't have the answers, and why they can't just make it go away like they are supposed to do. I am wondering about the black spot meteorite falling towards me, growing bigger and blacker as its shadow lands on my days. I am wondering what it feels like to have a real problem, when it is so hard, and so lonely and so scary just to have the unknown. Very lonely.

That day I talk to another girlfriend, who works with me at the hotel. She has been asking why all the doctor's appointments, so I tell. I tell her the whole story about the first mammogram, what's-his-name's wife, the toothpick man and the music video. She laughs and says there's nothing wrong with me. I say, "I don't know yet."

"Wait a minute," she says. She pulls a mail order catalogue out of her desk—fancy resort clothes and bathing suits. "I want to show you something in here." She flips through to the right page then covers the picture up with her hand.

"This is exactly what you need," she says. Her mouth quivers on one side as she opens the catalogue with an uncontrollable grin. It is a bathing cap, one of those remarkable rubber ones with flowers in pink, blue, yellow and bright green, blooming all over this beatific model's smiling head.

It is too much. We laugh and laugh and laugh. We look around the room. We visualize the fat security guard sporting one, and the bitchy office manager with her head abloom. We can see her boss wearing one in a meeting, and my boss with cigar and one. Our hysterics grow. We picture the grounds guys cutting the grass in these things, the golf pro trying to make a serious putt, and the pool boys winking at girls beneath their cranial bouquets.

It is a good enough laugh to sustain the whole day, and every time we see someone new we go into weeping, snorting giggle fits all over again. It is a miraculous thing. It is the funniest thing in the world. It is a huge blessing.

By the end of the day my eyes are swollen and my face is sore from laughing. I can't wait to show my husband the picture (He was already visualized with wrench and rubber bathing cap) with our sunset beers. He gets to laughing too, and we carry on 'til dark, imagining his supervisor, my Mom and all our old friends, lined up. We laugh and laugh until the moon comes up.

Then I remember.

"Oh by the way," I say. "I have to consult with a surgeon now."

"When?" he says.

"Next week."

"It's nothing, like I said," he said.

My first friend still insists that she loves the doctor trips, and even though we have to wait a long time, with or without the soap opera, we get to catch up and gossip a little without the kids or the men around.

I take the catalogue picture out of my purse and we laugh until she too nearly wets herself at the rubber bathing cap. "Can you see Steve in one of those?" she says, wiping her eyes. We mentally crown the doctors, all the nurses, and her mother-in-law. We tell the receptionist we don't mind the wait when she says the surgeon is delayed. We go out for lunch and come back.

The surgeon is a little man, even smaller than the radiologist. He would look great in a rubber bathing cap. He too scrutinizes the right tit, but without benefit of machines. His office does not have dolphins on the walls or scarves on the lampshades. After a little poking and kneading, he reads my file and asks when the first day of my last period was. "Yesterday," I say. It finally changed. He makes a note.

"You can get dressed now. I'll be right back," he says.

I get dressed and he comes back with the radiologist and my doctor. The Tit Committee is looking very serious and professional. I haven't put on my shoes yet. This is it, I guess, and me still barefoot.

"You should come back in a year for another mammogram," one of them says.

"What?"

"We find nothing to be concerned about at this time and you should come back in a year."

"A year?" I say. "Not six months?"

"A year," one of them says, "will be fine."

Far away, the meteorite gets caught in the earth's orbit. It stops its descent and hangs out with the satellites, its shadow moving quickly across the continents, faster than you can think.

They leave. My girlfriend looks anxious when I come out. "What?" she asks.

"I have to come back in a year."

"That's it?"

"That's it."

My husband, over his cigar, nods confidently.

"Aren't you glad I'm not dying of breast cancer?" I ask.

"I knew you weren't," he says. That's it.

"So what was it all about?" asks my bathing-cap girlfriend at work the next day.

"I'm not sure," I say.

Now every August, when my birthday goes by and it's time to put another mammogram on the calendar, I'm still not sure what it's all about. For Reality's tits, it's about measuring the baseline against any new developments and following up anomalies with further procedures.

For me, it's about remembering that first, strange time and the coincidental things I learned about healing that had nothing to do with Reality or her tits. I learned that Japanese women drink tonic from a magic mushroom that has babies if you take care of it. I learned that friends manage to be there when you need them the most, and that a blessing is a favor you don't have to repay. I learned the funniest thing in the whole wide world is a flower-covered rubber bathing cap.

And I learned how big eight millimeters is.

HONOLULU HOU
(New Honolulu)

I t is said that in the last days of the twenty-first century, there was only one reason to visit Honolulu Hou, and that was to eat.

As the exhausted planet slowly rolled over into a cycle of rest and cleansing, at least some of the old experts' theories began to prove themselves. The great glaciers, defrosting for one hundred years like turkeys in a bathtub, melted into the oceans, pushing sea level up and up, flooding into the human-occupied neighborhoods of the coastal world. The people retreated inward, as the farmers had retreated northward searching for cooler temperatures and enough rain to grow food. It might have worked if governments had not interfered, and imposed the invisible boundaries that defined the fiction of ownership, the illusion of control.

Reaction was slow at first, then accelerated with the force of panic as everything familiar shifted, turned and skewed like a hall of mirrors in some dark carnival. And as more and more of the people's concentration and energy focused on obtaining and consuming food, there was less and less. The one real mirror at the end of the hall showed them empty fields, empty pantries, empty stomachs.

Of course cooperation was finally the answer, but anthropologists can only guess from fragmented clues the number of dead. Famine, floods and *tsunami*, contamination and the terrible things that men will do to each other, a hundred new diseases from a hundred new viruses born in the new world condition, all took a piece of the humanity pie. It was a terrible tuition, but the survivors graduated knowing how to work together, and prepared a future to serve to another generation.

While all this was happening, the great chefs of the world, somehow as a single mind, decided that one day people would be able not just to eat, but to eat well again; the chefs determined that there would be a place on earth where their art would not just be preserved but propagated. With complete commitment to an unimagined community, they sold restaurants and wineries, bakeries, breweries and kitchen sinks. They bought the cherished visas and the last tickets for the last ships with the last civilian oil. And so, like missionaries 300 years before, with their pots and knives and their children, their grape stock, spices and seeds and priceless recipes, they began to gather in Honolulu Hou, in the Kingdom of Hawai'i.

It was one of those famous mornings, from the moment sunlight first poured like warm honey over the Ko'olaus, when the air was rich with delicious brightness and the smells of breakfast. Keoki sometimes thought he was full just from breathing in the essences of baking sweetbread, Big Island bacon, indescribable fruits, and the underlying constant Kona coffee everywhere.

It was his job to select the catch of the day for his father's restaurant. For ten of his twelve years, his father had taken him through the market himself, introducing him to the finer points of fish excellence. Looking into their glassy eyes and patting shiny skins, he learned to choose the best and to argue the best price, until now he was entrusted to do the job on his own.

Today there was fine *'ahi*, and Keoki was happy that his father would be happy. Tonight Poppa would make *sashimi*, as only he could, cutting up the *'ahi* on the big center table like a famous surgeon performing for medical students—making a big show of reducing the huge fish to elegant little slices. Keoki loved to watch his father at work.

He hurried along Ala Wai Beach from the Old Mall Wharf, waving quickly to the fruit vendors and the juice man, the Frenchman's half-Mexican daughter at Café Olé, the old Italian sweeping the sidewalk of the Impastable Dream, the *poi* pounder already drawing a couple of guests to Komo Mai's.

"Eat well, Keoki!" they called to him as he passed.

"Eat well," he replied.

He started up Kalākaua, and crossed the street at Kapi'olani to avoid the Christian leaflet-passers at The Last Supper, but realized at the next corner that it wasn't necessary. The corner was empty; the doors were closed. Just as his father and the other chefs had been saying, there was no way they could stay in business serving nothing but dates and unleavened bread with their hefty portions of gospel.

He rushed now past the familiar alphabet of shops that supported the restaurants, from Aprons, Baking Tins, Candles, Dishes to Silverware, Tablecloths and Ultra-violet Lights. As he passed, awnings rolled out, curtains opened, lights came on inside and everywhere menus bloomed in the windows and the city stood ready for the day's eating.

At last Keoki reached the drive-in where his father and mother were waiting, drinking their coffee with Mr. Chan, the noodle man. Of course there was nothing to *drive* in anymore, unless you were lucky enough to qualify for a royal truck lease, but they had built the place from an old movie scene. The neighbors all sat at their favorite tables and gave their favorite orders to radio boxes on the umbrella pole. Seconds later a waiter on roller skates swooped in with a steaming pot of coffee and sped back to the kitchen to grab his next order.

"Pop!" Keoki cried as he ran up to their table, "Pop, guess what I heard at the fish market!" His father sipped then stirred more sugar into his cup.

"What did you get?" he asked.

"*'Ahi*, but Pop . . ."

"Just a minute, I'm talking. As I was saying, Paolo, it will be a fabulous New Year. He's opening the last Château Lafitte Rothschild '98 and the very first Hilo Rain Burgundy. Incredible!"

"Poppa." A waitress Keoki's age gave him a grin as she set pancakes and steaming sweet coffee and milk in front of him.

"Just the way you like it, huh Keoki?" He ignored her and she rolled away giggling, "Eat well today!"

"Now, what?" his father finally asked, turning to face Keoki.

"They saw the lights again!" he said between mouthsful, "last night, just before the boats came in."

"Don't be silly. They're just trying to scare you so you don't pay attention. What did you pay for the *'ahi*?"

"Four lunches, one dinner for the owner."

"Very good." The father went back to his conversation with Paolo Chan, and Keoki turned to his pancakes. There were five exactly saucer-sized perfect *taro*-batter cakes. One of each:

coconut, pineapple, macadamia nut, mango and Moloka'i chocolate. He ate them as he did every morning, from least to most favorite, listening to the talk of wines under the blue sky and wondering about the lights.

After breakfast, Keoki and his mother went to their place to begin preparations for lunch. Theirs was only a local carry-out counter until the front doors opened for dinner at six o'clock sharp, but from the back porch, they served by all accounts the best international *bentos* on the island. *Bentos* were the butter & egg trade for the spouses of the Council of Chefs. They traded lunches for breakfast, lunches for wine, lunches with the milk-man, the rice man, the flower lady and the butcher, through some remarkable, and as yet incalculable for Keoki, system of home economics.

Today, the *'ahi* arrived with two employees of the Old Mall Wharf. They sat outside under the *lychee* tree and were treated to samples of the little off-track neighborhood's best: Sam Lee's Thai beef salad, John Johnson's soft Maui onion rings, Mrs. Nishigi's *nori sushi*, some *kung pao* chicken wings from Pake Kitchen and homemade Spam. Keoki's mother made unquestionably the best Spam in town, from an old unwritten recipe her grandmother had painstakingly produced and passed down.

As the men ate their *bentos*, Keoki stole away from his pot-washing to listen to that favorite male pastime, talking story. They remembered and repeated, topped, exaggerated and repeated again the stories of the fish they used to catch, the whales they used to see, the killer surf in winter, the killer bikinis basting themselves on the beach in summer, before the ozone thing, before the new wind thing. And today, above all else, they talked about the mysterious lights.

"Well, if it's a storm, Jimmy, I tell you it's the damndest storm these guys ever saw over there, and they been fishing these waters twenty years!" proclaimed Carlton Lindsey. Jimmy ate his Spam and shook his head.

"Do you think it's a storm, Uncle?" asked Keoki. Jimmy chewed, shrugged.

"I think it must be a ship way out to sea," said Carlton.

"But," Keoki persisted, "if it's a ship, why don't they call us on the radio?"

"Maybe the radio broke. Maybe the ship's on fire."

"But, why don't they come into port?"

"Maybe she's drifting this way on the new current, full of dead bodies. Maybe she's a ghost ship!" He winked slyly at Keoki.

"There's no such thing as ghosts!" Keoki protested.

"Well, it could be a space ship," stated Jimmy, swallowing, "some kind UFO."

Keoki whispered, "What they doing over here?"

"Trying to pick up *bentos*—but no more place for park!" The men laughed and ate some more, continued with their theories without noticing Keoki anymore.

"It's Captain Cook coming back."

"No. Lono. Lono coming back to take his islands back."

"It's a new volcano growing under the water. . . ."

Keoki didn't think any of it was funny. He turned his red face away and walked as dignified as he could back to the kitchen to finish his pots. Who cared anyway? They were just stupid lights in the stupid sky.

Keoki's mother, Lili, was a soft and patient woman and she loved her child fiercely—so much so that she couldn't imagine the days when families were permitted more than one, when a mother might have to divide her love. She was born on Kaua'i and learned hard work and strength in her father's rice paddies. At eighteen she sailed to Honolulu Hou to find a husband as the law suggested, and that was Washington Ha'aheo Yamashita. He was one of those combustibly creative chefs, quite literally some days when the lid blew off some new concoction and everyone had to scramble out of the kitchen while Poppa swore in Hawaiian-English-Japanese and put the fires out.

He could happily trace his lineage back to the original Council of Chefs on his grandfather's side, and to pre-Council days on the Hawaiian grandmother's side, both of which he proudly displayed in big charts on his restaurant's walls. He learned the art of cutting fish from his father when he was very young. He had stood at the elbow of his grandfather listening to countless debates during the Council's early days, as they created the recipe for the amazing stew that was to be their new society.

Ha'aheo listened and memorized the stories and told enraptured Keoki and his friends again and again—about the young King of Hawai'i, desperate to keep his people alive in the middle of the changing, frightened Pacific; about the great Chefs cooking for him, incredible food invented from whatever was left, in the days when nobody knew if the fish was safe, the days after Pearl Harbor disappeared in the flood, in the days when water was always boiled and nobody knew if the stories about the secret hidden nukes were true, and if they were, where?

The King and his advisors who stayed behind and the *Kupuna* and the Chefs sat at table together and ate and talked and cooked the future. And when it came time for the people to choose, they too were brave and voted to establish the Council of Chefs to administer the business of food, and they voted to use their lands and their energies to support the King's plan. They found comfort in work as they always had, planting vegetables on the golf courses and turning the lesser resorts into dairy and poultry farms. It happened not without difficulty, not without resistance, but slowly it happened, while the seas, as slowly, ground down the streets of old Waikīkī and constructed the new beaches of Honolulu Hou.

Keoki never grew tired of the story. He believed in the power of food to bring people together, especially great food and great people. He believed in his father and he believed in the role he would assume in his footsteps. He was happy and complete in his life, and did not approve of mysteries that interfered, like these unexplained lights the fishermen saw.

"What do you think they are, Ma?" Keoki asked his mother. She nodded, took the pen out of her mouth and wrote "salt," then looked up and smiled at her son's troubled face.

"What what are?"

"The lights, Ma, the ones the fishermen saw this morning. Do you think it's another ghost ship?"

"No. What do you mean another?"

"Like in the bad times when boats tried to get here from other countries but they all died."

"You've been listening to too many stories at the fish market."

"But I have to know what they are!"

"They're nothing. Do you want to go shopping with me?"

"No." He regretted the word, for shopping today would mean a trip to the Kapi'olani Salt Works, which some of the old folks still called the Park. It was one of his best adventures—even with his mother along—past the tent city and the old convention center ruins at Ala Wai Golftown, through the marshes and past the oyster beds to the flats and the magic work of coaxing salt out of the ocean. It would be a shame to miss it, but he had another idea.

"I'll do the garden." Lili understood, nodded again, gathered her list and bags into his old red wagon and gave him a quick kiss. "Eat well today, Mama," he said.

"Eat well, son."

Near 'Iolani Palace, the City Garden began, planted by the King himself in the beginning and faithfully tended by his subjects since, under the guardian eye of the imposing statue of King Kamehameha the Great. The garden had spread and evolved with the cravings of the gardeners. Although it would never replace the rich produce farms on the leeward coasts, it was a convenient source of fresh fruits, herbs, vegetables and flowers in exchange for work. It was a place where even the poorest could find a bite to eat well, and a symbol of hope and pride for the community. Keoki signed in with the *Luna* for two hours/ten pounds, and for two hours enjoyed the dirt in his hands, the satisfaction of straight, weedless rows and the warm sweet strawberries that left their evidence on his face like lipstick kisses.

"I need to see the King," he said to the *Luna* as he weighed in his basket and rinsed his feet and hands at the spigot.

"What for?" asked the *Luna*, tossing an extra couple bananas on the scale to check off ten pounds.

"I want to know about the lights in the sky that the fishermen see."

"He can't tell you," the *Luna* replied with an adult smile.

"Why not?"

"He just can't."

"I won't tell anybody! I won't mess up any secret plans. I won't make trouble about it!"

The *Luna* laid a hand on Keoki's head, turning his eyes to face his own, and spoke to them directly, sincerely, "He doesn't know."

It was a long moment of staring and thinking before Keoki was able to understand. When finally the *Luna* released his head with a little shake for emphasis, he felt like the thought had been rubbed into his scalp: *he didn't know*. Keoki picked up his basket and walked straight to the Palace door.

"I want to see the King, " he said to the guard.

"Eat well today, Sir. Do you have an appointment?" asked the tall, unbending man.

"No, but I have to see him. I have to ask him a question."

"I'm sorry, Sir."

Keoki drew himself up as tall as he could. "I am Keoki, son of Washington Ha'aheo Yamashita of the Council of Chefs, and I have the Charter right to ask the King a question with food in my hands." He held the basket straight out and bowed deeply. The guard did not laugh on the outside. He only extended his arm to push open the huge door that seemed to say "shhh" as he did. Keoki kicked off his slippers and stepped inside where an equally tall butler stood.

"This is Keoki, son of Washington Ha'aheo Yamashita of the Council of Chefs, invoking his Charter right to ask the King a question with food in his hands," announced the guard. Without a word, the butler took the basket and motioned Keoki to follow him. They walked down a long corridor, bright with windows and vases of flowers, around a corner and through an open-air passage to an ornamental iron gate. Keoki's heart pounded as they walked, and when the butler clanged back the latch, revealing a stone path into the garden, he had to catch his breath.

They were back in the garden. The *Luna* was there, still peace-fully pulling weeds. The butler passed the basket to the *Luna*, saying, "Your Majesty, this young man is from Council of Chefs, and is invoking his Charter right to ask the King a question." Keoki was stunned; he couldn't speak; he could only nod his head.

The King spoke softly and kindly, "I said the King didn't know, son." He returned the basket. Keoki gripped the handle and ran frightened, barefoot and unthinking down the King's

Street. *He didn't know, he didn't know* drummed in his head like eggs beaten in a bowl, running words with his footsteps, *he didn't know, he didn't know*. He ran and ran as if fear and ignorance were both chasing him and betting who would catch him first. He ran through the nasty alleys of the Ke'eaumoku Marketplace, smoking and sizzling with mysterious cook fires and ancient cooks arguing over potions of incredible concoction, their stalls a mess of roots and herbs and animal parts. A one-eyed vendor of indeterminable nationality or gender grinned over pots of strange and nauseating teas. Dark doorways creaked open to strains of dark music through beaded curtains and, somehow hanging in the trees, a club called Aphrodiscotheque flashed a crackling, hissing neon sign, "Today Chocolate Climax."

He ran past the Filling Station, where the pumps rang up beer by the liter to oilcloth booths on a black garage floor. He ran by Animal House where people sat at tables with their dogs and cats. He ran through the doors of his father's restaurant like a gust of wind, billowing the crisp whiteness of tablecloths and rattling the polished silver, the cherished china.

"Pop!" he cried out, making the waiters pause in their preening of the stations. "Poppa!" His father emerged from the kitchen in a steamy cloud of cooking fragrance, wiping his hands on his apron. "Poppa, please. I've asked everybody. I've asked the King himself but he didn't know. Poppa, what are the lights in the sky?"

Washington Ha'aheo Yamashita looked at his dirty, panting son, weakly clinging to a basket of strawberry stain. He looked around his restaurant slowly, proudly, and where his glance fell, the room came back to life as waiters turned to their set up and cooks to their stirring and tasting. Even the big *'ahi* resting on his ice bed in the center of the room seemed to straighten up and get back to the business of preparations for dinner. He took his son by the shoulder and steered him up the creaking metal stairs towards his office, high above the street where once people had watched for rescue ships or enemies. He talked as they climbed. "After you bathe, make sure your big knife is very sharp, because tonight you will help me with the *'ahi*." They reached the landing and sat together on the big wooden bench, where Keoki had not been the only one to wait for Mr. Yamashita's discipline.

"Do you see any lights, Keoki?" he asked.

"No," he sniffed, "it's day time."

"But you think they're out there, yeah?"

"Yes. The boys say they are. The fishermen said they saw them. The King said he doesn't know. Why doesn't somebody go and find out?" He rubbed a dirty hand across his nose.

"Nobody's going to go, because then they wouldn't have anything to talk about. It's too far away and we have too much work to do to go sailing away and try look for something that might be nothing."

"Why?"

"Because then you won't have anything to do when you grow up!" Ha'aheo was running out of patience. The day's menu of aromas drifted up the stairs, a sauce perhaps overcooking, reminding him. "I'm going to tell you the truth now. But you have to promise not to be afraid of it, no matter what. And stop asking everybody else, because everybody is going to tell you something different. OK?"

They looked out to sea together a moment as it prepared to receive the sun, now on its final descent. "OK," said Keoki seriously.

"It's the future, son, that's all."

"But what does it mean?"

"Nobody knows. It's not our business to know." He started down the steps, back to his kitchen. "It's our business to cook."

Keoki looked at the ocean. Behind him, rain crept over the Ko'olau in liquid clouds leading twilight into the valley. Keoki watched the reddening sun, like a perfect scoop of sorbet on a far flat plate of blueberry coulis. He wasn't happy with his father's answer, but he wasn't afraid.

It is said that in the last days of the twenty-first century, there was only one reason to visit Honolulu Hou, and that was to eat, and to eat well.

Author's Notes on Glossary

Hawaiian words used here are derived from what we know of the oral language brought to the islands by Polynesian explorers. Naturally, new words were added to describe their new surroundings and the plants and animals they encountered. The written form of this language was developed by Christian missionaries hundreds of years later, and incorporated many anglicized words for things that did not exist prior to their arrival. Present-day Hawaiian may be many miles away from its source, however the beautiful sound and poetic symbolism of this ancient language are still very much alive, and the words are used with respect.

Pidgin words and expressions in the stories come from a developing contemporary way of speaking. Some linguists believe Hawai'i pidgin is a language created by children. It is a combination of Hawaiian, Japanese, Chinese, Portuguese, Korean, Spanish, the Filipino languages, English and even make-believe, which plantation children from these various ethnicities came up with during play. It is the "potluck" of speech, which is very much en vogue among current Hawai'i writers. Whether it is a separate language or not, it is definitely more than slang, and a great deal of fun.

"Local" refers to a lifestyle here. Local words are those you might not hear on the mainland, but they are neither Pidgin nor Hawaiian. They include not only food (plate lunch), but dress (rubber slippers), music (slack key), humor and our uniquely practical way of giving directions (ocean-side and mountain-side). They also embrace whomever and whatever come here and include that in the mix. "Local" language is more than a regional flavor, it is a special blend of elements that make Hawai'i rich in taste and endlessly, diversely appealing to everyone who lives here, who visits, or who visits and stays.

'AHI

(<u>ah</u>-hee) *Thunnus albacares* Hawaiian word for various tuna, usually the yellow-fin. If raw fish can be beautiful, think of just-caught ahi, ruby red and glistening, cut to a perfect block and ready to slice into thin little jewels on your plate. Then it melts in your mouth like a combination of the perfect steak and the perfect tomato.

ANTHURIUM

genus Anthurium Tropical plant with heart-shaped, usually bright red flowers and long, distinctive stamen/anther.

ALI'I

(ah-<u>lee</u>-ee) Hawaiian word for royalty, revered persons.

'AUANA

(ow-<u>ah</u>-nah) Hawaiian word meaning to wander, or to stray morally. Presently most often a word for "modern" as in hula 'auana. Something that's "wandered" away from its source. Like fiction based on reality.

'AUMAKUA

(<u>ow</u>-mah-koo-ah) Hawaiian word for protective, ancestral spirits. Family gods that can assume shapes of animals or objects.

BAGASSE

(bah-<u>gas</u>) Dry pulp remaining from sugar cane after the juice has been extracted. From a Spanish word, "bagazo," meaning dregs.

BAMBOO SHOOTS

family Gramineae Tender, edible shoots of the bamboo. A frequent vegetable ingredient in Asian cuisine.

BENTO

(<u>ben</u>-toh) Japanese origin; a box lunch. Rice and a variety of other food, such as fried chicken, strips of beef, some vegetable. The box itself is usually segmented so the dishes don't mix; chopsticks and a packet of shoyu are usually inside.

BROTHERS CAZIMERO, THE

Contemporary Hawai'i singing duo; affectionately referred to as the Brothers Caz or "The Caz." A benchmark of modern local music.

BUMBYE
Pidgin word, loosely "by and by." In conversation it means "pretty soon" or "maybe later."

CAPT. JAMES COOK
English explorer who accurately pinpointed the Hawaiian Islands that he named the Sandwich Islands. The town in South Kona where he was killed at Kealakekua Bay in 1779 is named after him.

CHAR SIU
(char <u>see</u>-oo) Chinese origin; a bright red barbecue sauce made of water, sugar, salt, shoyu and seasonings. Stains everything, worse than strawberry Jell-O.

CHICKEN HEKKA
A chicken stew of Japanese origin made with mung bean noodles (long rice) and assorted vegetables. Authentic cooks swear you do not add beer. Also known as chicken long rice.

CHICKEN SKIN
Local version of goose bumps.

CRACK SEED
Local treat made of dried, salted and/or sugared fruit such as plum, mango, lemon peel, cranberries and other unidentifiable substances. (See li hing mui.) The really sour ones feel like they can remove dental enamel.

CUTTLEFISH
Sepia officinalis Marine mollusk; meat is dried and eaten as a snack. Resembles dried up chewing gum and does not taste like anything that could have been alive.

DAI-ZEN
A local fast food place without the burgers and shakes. Plate lunches, potluck stuff to go.

DIM SUM
A whole category of Chinese treats; different-shaped steamed dumplings filled with various meats, seafood and vegetables. Lumpy little delicious things that make it worthwhile to learn to eat with chopsticks.

'ELEPAIO
(eh-lay-<u>pai</u>-oh) *Chasiempis sandwichensis* Hawaiian word for species of flycatcher with subspecies on Hawai'i, Kaua'i and O'ahu.

FATHER DAMIEN
Hawai'i historical figure. A Catholic priest who made his life work helping the victims of Hansen's disease also known as leprosy on Moloka'i.

FERN SHOOTS
Very young shoots of a warabi fern, steamed forever to remove the hairs, then served like asparagus or in salads.

FISHCAKE
Kamaboko. We think this is reconstituted, ground-up white fish and cornstarch, rolled into a cylinder and dyed pink on the outside. We can't be sure. Served with a little green fringe.

FURIKAKE
(foo-ree-<u>kah</u>-kay) A flavoring agent of roastred seaweed, salt, sesame seeds and other ingredients, often sprinkled atop rice.

GOBO
(goh-<u>boh</u>) Burdock root, boiled and served like turnips. If it's brownish and you can't identify it any other way, ask if it's gobo.

HALEMA'UMA'U
(<u>hah</u>-lay-<u>mah</u>-oo-<u>mah</u>-oo) The largest crater in Hawai'i Volcanoes National Park. Some believe it to be Pele's home.

HANSEN'S DISEASE
Proper medical designation for the disease known as leprosy.

HAOLE
(<u>how</u>-lay) Hawaiian word meaning literally "no breath." Thought to come from a Hawaiian custom of breathing close to a person's cheek in greeting. Foreigners of course did not do this. It also has a spiritual connotation and so indicated a lack of spirit in the strangers. Used presently to mean a Caucasian person.

HAWAIIAN BABY LŪ'AU
Local custom of throwing a huge party for baby's first birthday usually

serving Hawaiian food, but always serving enormous amounts of everything. Note for newcomers: Do not invest time in selecting a tasteful gift. Put money in an envelope.

HAWAIIAN SUN
One standard local brand of canned, sweetened fruit drink made in Hawai'i. Comes in tropical flavors such as guava, mango, passion fruit.

HEAHEA
(hay-ah-hay-ah) Hawaiian word, to welcome, to call frequently and hospitably. "He leo heahea," a welcoming voice.

HI'ILAWE
(hee-ee-lah-vay) Hawaiian word meaning lit. to lift or carry. A legendary twin waterfall at the back of Waipi'o Valley in the Hāmākua district of the Big Island.

HOLOKŪ
(hoh-loh-koo) Hawaiian word for loose dress usually with a train. Possibly derived from holo (to run or to flow) because of the train. It's a more formal mu'u mu'u, usually floor-length, with a high, yoked neckline and long sleeves.

HONEY CREEPER
Vestiaria coccinea The most popular is the Hawaiian i'iwi, the scarlet honey creeper's feathers were used extensively in featherwork.

HOU
(hoh oo) Hawaiian word for new, fresh, recent. Also as in "hana hou," do it again. Say this at the end of a concert, and the band will play an encore.

HOWZIT
Pidgin for "How is it (going)?" A friendly greeting.

'IOLANI PALACE
(ee-oh-lah-nee) Historic location in Honolulu. The last home of Hawai'i's reigning monarchy.

KAHIKO
(kah-hee-koh)Hawaiian word for old, ancient, antique, primitive. Presently used to describe traditional, authentic hula (as opposed to

"'auana," or modern.)

KAHU

(<u>kah</u>-hoo) Hawaiian word meaning honored attendant, administrator. "Kahu" presently is almost the same as "Father," "Pastor" or "Teacher." It's a familiar title used with or without a surname.

KAHUNA

(ka-<u>hoo</u>-nah)Hawaiian word for priest or wizard. Also means expert in a field. There are as many different kinds of kahuna as there are fields to study—healing, casting spells, performing rituals, teaching, artworks. Some believe the word is from ka (the) huna (secret), making these people the "keepers of the secrets."

KĀLUA PIG

(kah-<u>loo</u>-ah) Whole pig baked in a pit, or ground oven (imu). To "kalua one pig" is the present day version of the "imu ceremony." It means take the weekend off, get all the guys together, dig a hole, line it with stones, set a kiawe-wood fire, watch it burn down to coals, throw in some banana stumps to make steam, set the pig (wrapped in chicken wire) in the hole and drink beer all night for safety reasons. The next day you dig it up and eat it. The parts that stick to the chicken wire are the best.

KAMABOKO

(kah-mah-<u>boh</u>-koh) See fishcake.

KA MAKANI

(kah mah-<u>kah</u>-nee) Hawaiian words meaning lit. the wind. Virtually every type and location of the wind has its own name.

KIAWE

(kee-<u>ah</u>-vay) *Prosopis pallida* Hawaiian word for the Algaroba tree, originally from Peru, very similar to mainland mesquite. Lit. to sway, as branches in the breeze. A scrubby tree found in dry areas; branches used for cooking with fire. Some have armor-piercing, non-poisonous, foot-seeking thorns. Don't walk with rubber slippers under that kind.

KIM CHEE

Of Korean origin, it is a very spicy fermented vegetable (usually cabbage).

KLINGON
A race of alien characters from the "Star Trek" series. Warrior-types who eat living things.

KOA
(<u>koh</u>-ah) *Acacia koa* Hawaiian word for strong. Also, the largest of ancient native forest trees with light gray bark, crescent shaped leaves. It was used to make canoes. The wood is highly prized for furniture, jewelry, etc.

KUNG PAO CHICKEN
Chinese dish of chicken and cashews in a dark, very peppery sauce.

KUPUNA
(koo-<u>poo</u>-nah) Hawaiian word for grandparent, elder, wise one. Also means source or starting point.

LEI
(layeh) Hawaiian word for garland, a necklace of flowers, leaves, nuts, seeds or shells. A symbol of festivity and honor for any special occasion. Never throw a lei away. Burn it; toss it in the ocean. If you enjoyed your stay at a particular hotel, hang it on the doorknob, and maybe you'll come back someday. Before airplane travel, lei were thrown from the ship for the same reason.

LI HING MUI
(lee hing <u>moo</u>-ee) Chinese origin; A type of crack seed, distinguished by the use of li hing mui powder as flavoring. This fine red powder contains licorice, aspartame, and secret ingredients that make it taste sweet, sour, spicy and salty at the same time. Its use as a component of Margaritas is presently under experimentation.

LOCO MOCO
A local delicacy, adapted by "Cafe 100" in Hilo from dock workers' fare and now served all over the islands. Two scoops of rice in a bowl, hamburger patty topped with a fried egg and gravy. Once you try it, your arteries will never forget it.

LONG RICE
Also called "bean thread." Clear noodles made from mung beans, of Chinese origin. Innocuous in the bag. Very Klingon-esque after a cou-

ple of minutes in water. Used in chicken hekka. Nearly impossible to eat with a fork.

LONO
(lone-oh) One of the four principal Hawaiian deities brought to the islands. Lono represents agriculture, clouds and weather.

LŪ'AU PLATES
(loo-ow) Acceptable tableware for potluck, barbecues or lū'au. Large, sectioned cardboard plates, specifically designed for serving foods with liquid. Never round; usually safest to use two together.

LUNA
(loo-na)Hawaiian word for over, above, etc. Used as title for supervisor, foreman, leader, boss.

MACAW
Ara or *Andorhynchus* Species of large tropical bird originally from South America. Bright colored plumage with long tails and large, powerful beaks. Contrary to popular belief, their diet consists of fruits, nuts and vegetables, not human fingers.

MAHALO
Hawaiian word for thanks, gratitude.

MAILE
(mai-lay) *Alyxia olivaeformis* Hawaiian native twining shrub; its fragrant vine and leaves make a popular lei, usually open-ended. It is used for grand openings of homes and businesses, weddings (usually worn by the groom), graduations, blessings and other auspicious occasions. Long maile lei are ceremonially un-tied to open a building or event, like a ribbon-cutting.

MAI TAI
A drink concocted of a Kingston Jamaican rum in the '40s by Vic of Trader Vic's, an Oakland restaurant. His first taste testers were friends visiting from Tahiti who exclaimed "mai tai roa ae" (roughly "it's the best") after tasting. It has been called Mai Tai since.

MAKAI
(mah-kai) Hawaiian word for a direction, lit. at or towards the sea.

MALIHINI

(mah-lee-<u>hee</u>-nee) Hawaiian word for stranger, foreigner, newcomer. It is not true that it is always preceded by "stupid."

MANA

(<u>mah</u>-nah) Hawaiian word for supernatural or divine power.

MANAPUA

(mah-nah-<u>poo</u>-ah) Local version of one type of dim sum. From, mea ono pua'a, lit. pig cake; steamed dumpling of shredded pork wrapped in a soft dough. One of the best things in the world, highly addictive, known to cause sudden, impulsive stops at Chinese bakeries on the way to Honolulu Airport.

MAUKA

(<u>mau</u>-kah) Hawaiian word for a direction, lit. at or towards the mountains.

MAUNA KEA

(<u>mau</u>-nah <u>kay</u>-ah) Lit. "white mountain" because it is occasionally snow-capped. Mauna Kea is the highest mountain peak on the planet, when measured from the ocean floor. It is also a site for a growing international community of astronomical observatories.

MEJIRO

family Zosteropidae A small green bird from Japan, now common on all the islands. Bright and quick. Also known as round-eye or rice bird.

MENEHUNE

(<u>meh</u>-nay-<u>hoo</u>-nay) Hawaiian word for a race of mystical "little people" who worked during the night to build roads, fishponds, temples.

MENPACHI

(men-<u>pah</u>-chee) *Family Holocentridae* Squirrel fish. A small, red saltwater fish caught from the shoreline by line or net.

MISO SOUP

(<u>mee</u>-so) Japanese dish made with fermented red or white soybean paste. Served hot, usually with tofu and green onions.

MOCHI

(<u>moh</u>-chee) Japanese sweet made of rice. The traditional process is long and arduous, involving a lot of ceremonial preparation and pounding by a group of people. I think it takes a good two weeks to make your decent mochi. Currently done in the microwave. Or stop by "Two Ladies Kitchen" in Hilo and have some wrapped around a fresh strawberry. To die for.

MU'UMU'U

(moo-oo-<u>moo</u>-oo) Hawaiian word for a loose gown or chemise. Also means "cut off" or "amputated." Possibly from cutting the sleeves and yoke off a holoku. Caution: it is a well-known fact that the wearing of mu'umu'u causes the haole body to enlarge over time in order to fill the available space.

MUSUBI

(moo-soo-<u>bee</u>) Japanese derivation. A local snack, made of flavored rice usually wrapped in seaweed. A kind of rice "sandwich," with Spam, tuna or other filling smashed between two layers of rice in a lucite press, then rolled in a sheet of nori (seaweed). Sounds terrible. Tastes great.

NĒNĒ

(nay-<u>nay</u>) *Nesochen sandvicensis* A rare, protected Hawaiian goose usually found on Maui and Hawai'i uplands, but can thrive at sea level in protected areas. Believed to be descended from wayward Canada geese.

NORI

(<u>noh</u>-ree) Japanese origin; paper-thin, dried seaweed for eating. Used in sushi, musubi and other local and Asian foods.

OBAKE

(oh-<u>bah</u>-kay) Japanese word for ghost or spirit. It is also the name of a variety of large, showy anthurium flower.

'ŌHI'A LEHUA

(oh-<u>hee</u>-ah) *Metrosideros macropus* Hawaiian tree; one of the first plants to grow after a lava flow. Prized for bonzai gardening, and for its powder-puff red, yellow, orange and (rarely) white flowers. Very hard wood, great for floors.

OLD BAY SEASONING
A commercial spice mixture, originally from the Chesapeake Bay area of the eastern U.S., used to flavor shrimp, crabs, lobster or other boiled-in-shell seafood.

ONO
(<u>oh</u>-noh) *Acanthocybium solandri* Hawaiian fish, similar to mackerel. Called "wahoo" in the eastern U.S. 'Ono (with okina or glottal stop) means delicious. Ono certainly is.

O'O
(<u>oh</u>-oh) Hawaiian word for a stick used as a planting or digging tool; lit. to pierce, poke, put in, insert.

'ŌPAKAPAKA
(oh-<u>pah</u>-kah-<u>pah</u>-kah) *Pristipomoides sieboldii* Hawaiian fish, also known as crimson snapper. Delicious, white light-textured fish which can be prepared in many different ways.

'OPIHI
(oh-<u>pee</u>-hee) Hawaiian word for limpet. Looks like barnacle.

PAKALŌLŌ
(pah-kah-<u>loh</u>-loh) Hawaiian word for marijuana.

PALI
(<u>pah</u>-lee) Hawaiian word for cliff, precipice, steep hill.

PANIOLO
(pah-nee-<u>oh</u>-loh) Hawaiian word for cowboy; possibly from "Espanol" as early cattle drovers were Spanish-speaking Mexicans. Paniolo is a great combination of Hawai'i-Western lifestyle, very much alive in Waimea or Kamuela on the Big Island and areas of Maui.

PAU
(pow) Hawaiian word for finished, ended, through.

PAU HANA
(pow <u>hah</u>-nah) Hawaiian for "the work is finished." Pidgin phrase meaning "quitting time."

PEABERRY
Different from the normal two-sectioned coffee bean, the peaberry is a

smaller, solid bean. It is fuller flavored and rare; a typical harvest might have only one to five percent peaberries.

PELE

(pay-lay) Hawaiian volcano goddess, once feared, still very much revered. Also means volcano, eruption.

PETROGLYPH

A drawing carved into rock. Many well-preserved Hawai'i petroglyph sites are accessible on all the islands. Various interpretations have been applied from graffiti to religious symbols. What writers did before laptops. And please check out *Ki'i and Li'i: A Story from the Stones* also from Goodale Publishing.

PIETÀ

(pee-ay-tah) Theme of religious sculpture or painting; it shows Mary holding Jesus' adult body after his death. Michaelangelo's Pieta is one of the most famous representation of the theme. From Italian, lit., piety.

PIDGIN

A simplified form of speech, usually a mixture of two or more languages, that has a rudimentary grammar and vocabulary and is used for communication between groups speaking different languages.

PIKO

(pee-koh) Hawaiian for navel or umbilical cord, also the peak or summit of the mountain, the crown of the head.

POI

(poy) Hawaiian staple food, made with cooked taro root pounded and thinned with water to make a paste. Could be eaten fresh, or dried and stored for long periods of time. It's purple; it doesn't taste like anything else there is; it can be eaten with anything—from cream and sugar to lomi salmon or hot dogs—or all by itself. Some people let it sit until it's sour. To each his own poi.

POKE

(po-kay) Hawaiian word meaning lit. to cut into cubes. Poke, "Hawai'i's Soul Food" (Sam Choy), is a kind of fish salad, a combination of cut fish or seafood which can be raw, seared or cooked, then marinated and tossed with an unlimited variety of other ingredients and flavorings. Traditional poke was only made with sea salt, limu (seaweed) and fish, flavored with inamona (kukui nut relish).

PULAKAUMAKA

(poo-lah-kau-<u>mah</u>-kah) Hawaiian word for fixation or obsession, or a person one thinks of constantly.

PUNA

(<u>poo</u>-nah) Hawai'i Island rural district on the east side of the island, attractive to farmers and seekers of alternative lifestyles.

PŪ'OLO

(poo-<u>oh</u>-loh) Hawaiian word for container or parcel usually containing a gift of food or lei. An ingenious gift-wrapping for lei can be made with ti leaf. Tie a bundle of 10 or 12 leaves together by the stems, then set the bundle on a table so the leaves fan out all around and the stems make a center post. Wind your lei around the post. Then gather the leaves around and above that, and tie them at the top with raffia. Beautiful and keeps the lei fresh.

PU'U

(<u>poo</u>-oo) Hawaiian word for hill, rise, or any other protuberance.

PU'U HONUA O HŌNAUNAU

(<u>poo</u>-oo hoh-<u>noo</u>-ah oh <u>hoh</u>-oh-nau-nau) "Place of Refuge" in Hōnaunau in the South Kona district of the Big Island. A Hawaiian spiritual center; it is believed that a person who reached this place would be sheltered, regardless of his or her wrongdoings. Now a national historical site.

SAIMIN

(sī-min) A soup dish made of wheat noodles and broth, with a variety of ingredients floating around in it—fishcake, char siu, green onion. Zippy's Restaurants have perfected the art of saimin presentation. The slurping is up to you. (Rumors that saimin is only one noodle two miles long are unfounded.)

SALOON PILOT CRACKERS

Sweetened crackers made in Hawai'i by Diamond Bakery. A local snack food with cream cheese and red pepper jelly, guava jam and butter, or myriad other combinations. Available in five-gallon buckets.

SASHIMI
(sah-<u>shee</u>-mee) Of Japanese origin; sliced raw fish most often 'ahi (yellow fin tuna.) served with wasabi (Japanese hot green horseradish) and soy sauce.

SHAVE ICE
Local version of a "snow cone," a cool treat made from ice which is shaved off large blocks with a big machine, then flavored with very sweet syrup.

SHOYU
(<u>shoh</u>-yoo) Soy sauce. Sauce made of fermented soy beans. "Light" shoyu will not have as much molasses and/or corn syrup as "dark" shoyu, but both are heavy on the salt. Keep it on the table. Don't make people ask. (Something called "kecap" is the Indonesian name for shoyu—which might be where the American word "ketchup" comes from, since it was such a common condiment, served with every meal.)

SUSHI
(soo-<u>shee</u>) Believed to be of Chinese origin as long as 2000 years ago, perfected as an artform in Japanese cuisine; a category of snacks generally made with vinegar-seasoned rice, rolled and sliced, topped with a wide variety of raw fish, seafood and flavorings. Not to be confused with sashimi, which is just the fish.

TI
(tee) *Cordyline terminalis* The rarely used Hawaiian word is "ki." A woody plant in the lily family, extremely important to early Hawaiian life. Leaves were used for house thatch, food wrappers, hula skirts, sandals, etc. Many local good luck traditions involve ti. Plant green ti in the four corners of your yard. Carry a little piece of it next to your skin for blessing. Wear a ti-leaf lei for cleansing and healing, and to protect yourself from dark spirits (among other important reasons.)

TSUNAMI
(soo-<u>nah</u>-mee) Japanese origin. A very large ocean wave caused by undersea earthquake or a volcanic eruption. Often called tidal wave.

TŪTŪ
(too-too) The Hawaiian word is kūkū, but it is rarely used. Means granny, grandma, grandpa, grand aunt and grand uncle.

UNCLE BILLY'S SUNDAY BRUNCH BUFFET
Famous local breakfast buffet, served up at Uncle Billy's Hilo Bay or Kona Bay Hotels, noted for its variety of dishes and affordable price.

WASABI PEAS
(wah-<u>sah</u>-bee) Japanese origin; a snack made of dried peas covered in a wasabi (hot green horseradish) and cracker crust. There are levels of spiciness. Use caution; read the label.

WILIWILI
(wee-lee-<u>wee</u>-lee) *Erythrina sondicensis* Hawaiian tree found on dry coral plains and on lava flows. Very much a favorite of the mejiro bird. Spectacular red blooms once a year, just after you think it has died. The colorful seeds make great lei, necklaces.

BIBLIOGRAPHY

Nana I Ke Kumu (Look to the Source), Vol I and II, Mary Kawena Pukui, E.W. Haertig, MD, Catherine A. Lee; Publisher: Hui Hanai, An Auxiliary of the Queen Lili'uokalani Children's Center, Honolulu, 1972

Hawaiian Dictionary - Revised and Enlarged Edition, Mary Kawena Pukui, Samuel H. Elbert; University of Hawai'i Press, Honolulu, 1986

Craig Claiborne's *The New York Times Food Encyclopedia*; Wings Books (by arrangement with Times Books, a division of RandomHouse, Inc.), New York, 1994

Place Names of Hawai'i, Mary Kawena Pukui, Samuel H. Elbert, Esther T. Mookini, revised and expanded edition, University of Hawai'i Press, Honolulu, 1974

Reader's Digest Book of Facts, The Reader's Digest Association Inc., New York, 1987